AN AMISH THANKSGIVING (A ROMANCE)

INCLUDES AMISH RECIPES & READING GROUP GUIDE

BETH WISEMAN

To my family—those I was born to love and those I choose to love. You know who you are, and you are all my family.

ACCLAIM FOR BETH WISEMAN

The House That Love Built

"This sweet story with a hint of mystery is touching and emotional. Humor sprinkled throughout balances the occasional seriousness. The development of the love story is paced perfectly so that the reader gets a real sense of the characters."

~ ROMANTIC TIMES, 4-STAR REVIEW

"[The House That Love Built] is a warm, sweet tale of faith renewed and families restored."

~ BOOKPAGE

The Promise

Bestselling author Beth Wiseman (The House that Love Built) encourages readers to think through their feelings about Islam, Christianity, faith, love, and what it means to help others. Her novel will challenge, encourage, and stimulate discussion among her loyal fans and first-time readers.

~ Publishers Weekly

"Promises. Easy to make, far easier to break. Beth Wiseman tells a gripping story of promises, both made and broken. Mallory's journey, along with Tate, is one for the ages. The Promise is on my All-Star List."

~ Lis Wiehl, New York Times bestselling author

Need You Now

"Wiseman, best known for her series of Amish novels, branches out into a wider world in this story of family, dependence, faith, and small-town Texas, offering a character for every reader to relate to . . . With an enjoyable cast of outside characters, *Need You Now* breaks the molds of small-town stereotypes. With issues ranging from special education and teen cutting to what makes a marriage strong, this is a compelling and worthy read." ~ BOOKLIST

"Wiseman gets to the heart of marriage and family interests in a way that will resonate with readers, with an intricately written plot featuring elements that seem to be ripped from current headlines. God provides hope for Wiseman's characters even in the most desperate situations." ~ ROMANTIC TIMES, 4-STAR REVIEW

"You may think you are familiar with Beth's wonderful story-telling gift but this is something new! This is a story that will stay with you for a long, long time. It's a story of hope when life seems hopeless. It's a story of how God can redeem the seemingly unredeemable. It's a message the Church, the world needs to hear." ~ SHEILA WALSH, AUTHOR OF *GOD LOVES BROKEN PEOPLE*

"Beth Wiseman tackles these difficult subjects with courage and grace. She reminds us that true healing can only come by being vulnerable and honest before our God who loves us more than anything." ~ DEBORAH BEDFORD, BESTSELLING AUTHOR OF *HIS OTHER WIFE, A ROSE BY THE DOOR, AND THE PENNY* (COAUTHORED WITH JOYCE MEYER)

The Land of Canaan Novels

"Wiseman's voice is consistently compassionate and her words flow smoothly." ~ PUBLISHERS WEEKLY REVIEW OF *SEEK ME WITH ALL YOUR HEART*

"Wiseman's third Land of Canaan novel overflows with romance, broken promises, a modern knight in shining armor and hope at the end of the rainbow." ~ ROMANTIC TIMES

"In *Seek Me with All Your Heart*, Beth Wiseman offers readers a heart-warming story filled with complex characters and deep emotion. I instantly loved Emily, and eagerly turned each page, anxious to learn more about her past—and what future the Lord had in store for her." ~

SHELLEY SHEPARD GRAY, BESTSELLING AUTHOR OF *THE SEASONS OF SUGARCREEK SERIES*

"Wiseman has done it again! Beautifully compelling, *Seek Me with All Your Heart* is a heart-warming story of faith, family, and renewal. Her characters and descriptions are captivating, bringing the story to life with the turn of every page." ~ AMY CLIPSTON, BESTSELLING AUTHOR OF *A GIFT OF GRACE*

The Daughters of the Promise Novels

"Well-defined characters and story make for an enjoyable read." ~ ROMANTIC TIMES REVIEW OF *PLAIN PURSUIT*

"A touching, heartwarming story. Wiseman does a particularly great job of dealing with shunning, a controversial Amish practice that seems cruel and unnecessary to outsiders . . . If you're a fan of Amish fiction, don't miss *Plain Pursuit!*" ~ KATHLEEN FULLER, AUTHOR OF *THE MIDDLEFIELD FAMILY NOVELS.*

ALSO BY BETH WISEMAN

Listening to Love

A Beautiful Arrangement

An Amish Inn Series

A Picture of Love

An Unlikely Match

A Season of Change

An Amish Bookstore Series

The Bookseller's Promise

The Story of Love

Hopefully Ever After

Stand-Alone Amish Novel

The Amish Matchmakers

Short Stories/Novellas

An Amish Adoption

The Messenger

Return of the Monarchs

An Amish Christmas Gift

An Amish Healing Series

An Amish Healing

Ollie's Story: An Amish Healing Redux

Surf's Up Novellas

A Tide Worth Turning

Message In A Bottle

The Shell Collector's Daughter

Christmas by the Sea

GLOSSARY

ab im kopp: off in the head/crazy
   ach: oh
   braucherei: a type of folk magic originating in the culture of the Pennsylvania Dutch
   bruder: brother
   daed: dad
   danki: thank you
   Englisch: those who are not Amish
   fraa: wife
   Gott: God
   grossdaadi: grandfather
   grossmammi: grandmother
   gut: good
   haus: house
   kaffi: coffee
   kinner: children
   lieb/liebed: love/loved
   maedel/maeds: girl/girls
   mammi: short for grandmother

mei: my

mudder: mother

nee: no

Ordnung: unwritten rules of the Amish

schweschder/schweschdere: sister/sisters

sohn: son

wie bischt: hello/how are you?

ya: yes

CHAPTER 1

*C*atherine Lapp stood in the kitchen, closed her eyes, and imagined the aroma of turkey roasting in the oven. Her mouth watered as she thought about the bird defrosting in the refrigerator. When it was thawed, she would baste it in butter, then stuff it with celery, onions, and thyme, filling the old farmhouse with smells of the season.

For the fourth year in a row, Catherine would prepare the turkey, along with all the side dishes, for only her and her grandmother. Just three more days until their celebration. Just the two of them. It wasn't ideal, but it was her grandmother's favorite holiday, and Catherine would do her best to make it as festive as possible. She allowed herself to go back in time and remember the way the holiday table used to be set for a lot more people.

Her reflective moment was short-lived, and Catherine opened her eyes when she heard her grandmother calling for her. "Jessica, bring me some of that moonshine in the basement, will you, please?"

Catherine sighed as she shook her head. She had no idea why her grandmother had started to call her Jessica over the past couple of years. To Catherine's knowledge, they didn't even know anyone named Jessica, nor was it an Amish name. And her grandfather had been dead for over a decade. Catherine was pretty sure he'd never made moonshine, but she couldn't completely rule it out since she was only a child when he was alive.

She opened the refrigerator and took out a pitcher of strong meadow tea that she'd made earlier that morning, dark enough to pass for the moonshine her grandmother requested.

"Coming, *Grandmammi*." She poured the liquid into a blue plastic glass, added only two cubes of ice—as her grandmother always insisted—then dumped enough imitation sugar into the glass to pacify her.

Catherine shuffled toward the downstairs master bedroom where Catherine's parents used to live until four years ago—before their midlife crisis that had peaked in their forties. Sarah and Amos Lapp announced they were leaving their Amish community, then quickly filed for an English divorce. They left Catherine—then twenty-three years old—alone with her grandmother, who had been living with all of them since her grandfather passed.

Technically, her parents had been shunned, which banned Catherine from seeing or speaking to them. Occasionally, she bent the rules when she received letters from her mother and wrote back. Each time, her mother would inquire about her mother—Catherine's grandmother—but she never mentioned coming home, sometimes saying she wasn't allowed to return. Catherine wondered if that was just an excuse and if the bishop would have made an exception under the circumstances if her mother had inquired. As much as Catherine loved her grandmother, bitterness nipped at her heart about the choices her parents had made.

She hadn't heard anything from her father, and that was okay with her on most days. It was a known fact that her father had stepped out with other women, but when she recalled the man she remembered him to be during her childhood, it saddened her not to have a father figure in her life.

Although she had been guilty of judgment plenty of times, especially when her grandmother was having a rough day, it wasn't Catherine's place to judge her parents for their choices.

At twenty-seven and unmarried, Catherine had insisted on staying in the house where she'd grown up, in the community where she'd been baptized, and she remained adamant about her dedication to the *Ordnung*. Her parents hadn't argued about her choice to stay, and even seemed relieved. What would they have done if Catherine hadn't stayed? Who would have taken care of her grandmother? Catherine adored her grandma even on the challenging days. She didn't have any regrets.

Things changed after her parents departed. Folks didn't come around much except for two elderly sisters who ran a nearby bed and breakfast, The Peony Inn. Lizzie and Esther visited often. Her people preached love, compassion, and understanding, though Catherine felt that she had been shunned right along with her parents. Maybe it was partly her own doing. She'd grown weary of the whispers and strange looks when she was out and about, often overhearing references about her parents. Then, her grandmother's behavior became too unpredictable to chance a public embarrassment.

Catherine's mother and father had left not long after her grandmother's health began to decline. Dementia, the doctor called it. Catherine didn't leave the house anymore for fear her grandmother would inadvertently get hurt if left alone. Twice, the older woman had almost burned down the house when she'd tried to cook a meal while Catherine had gone out for a quick errand.

Hardest to bear was that Catherine missed worship service. The bishop visited at least twice a month, but Catherine sensed it was out of duty. Most of the time, her grandmother would offer the bishop moonshine or curse at him for events that only resided in her mind. *A beautiful, tortured mind.* Catherine missed her grandmother so much that she often cried herself to sleep. But there were also days of great joy when her grandmother was behaving normally. Those days were becoming more and more scarce, but Catherine cherished them.

As she scooted into the bedroom with the tea/moonshine, Catherine took a deep breath and prepared herself for whatever tale her grandmother might spin. Oh, how she loved this woman buried somewhere beneath a cruel disease that took her from reality to a place where Catherine was often Jessica and sometimes a total stranger.

"Here you go, *Mammi.*" Catherine placed the glass on the bedside table next to a box of tissues. Her grandmother's physicality was intact, as she had often reminded

Catherine when she'd tried to help her eat or drink anything, and she always insisted on bathing herself. Only her mind was failing, and with each day, it became harder to watch.

Her grandmother patted the bed, an invitation for Catherine to sit and visit.

"Are you feeling okay today, *Mammi?*" Catherine offered a weak smile and said a silent prayer that her grandmother's mind would be intact, even if just for today, despite the moonshine request.

The older woman shrugged, still in bed and wearing a white nightgown at ten in the morning. Her gray hair flowed past her waist, seeming to thin a little more as time marched on.

"*Ya,* I always feel okay." Then she smiled sweetly. Her wrinkles feathered from each eye and trailed vertically down her cheeks, meeting up with fine lines around her lips like a roadmap of the life she'd lived. She'd once told Catherine that for every wrinkle on her face, there was a story attached to it.

Her grandmother had always been a happy person, but these days, it was hit or miss. Right now, her eyes sparkled as she smiled, but within seconds, her mood could change faster than a derailed locomotive, throwing everything and everyone off track.

But the only time Mary Marie Byler showed genuine anger was when Catherine's parents abandoned them. Her grandmother screamed and hollered at her daughter. Catherine's mother, Sarah, had defended herself and said it was God's will that she and Catherine's father divorce and go their separate ways. Catherine didn't think it was

God's will for her parents to divorce, and she still struggled with it sometimes. If her grandmother harbored resentment, she never spoke of it.

"Today is Monday," her grandmother stated. "Do we have all the supplies we need for our Thanksgiving Day feast?" Her eyes still twinkling, she pressed her palms together.

So far, so good, Catherine thought as she nodded. "*Ya*, I think we have everything we need."

"*Gut*." Her grandmother raised her shoulders, her palms still pressed together as she smiled. "We're going to have a crowd this year."

Catherine's heart sank She knew it would only be the two of them, but she would play along. "I didn't realize that *Mammi*. Who is coming?" Forcing a smile, she braced herself for whatever crowd her grandmother was concocting in her mind.

"I have no idea." She giggled like a child with a secret. "*Gott* just told me that we are going to have a big Thanksgiving, so I want to make sure we have enough food."

Catherine swallowed back the knot building in her throat. "I'm sure we will," she said, barely above a whisper, willing her voice not to crack, and thinking how wonderful that would be . . . if only it was true.

"And last time I checked, we were out of potatoes." She pointed a crooked finger at Catherine, laughing again. "And *mei maedel*, we can't have Thanksgiving without potatoes."

Catherine widened her eyes in surprise. "*Ya*, you're right. We are out of potatoes." She kept canned potatoes in the basement for times she couldn't get to the store.

After they were mashed and seasoned, her grandmother couldn't tell the difference.

"And do you remember that recipe for pecan pie that your grandfather *liebed* so much?" Before Catherine could answer, she waved a dismissive hand. "You know the one. I haven't made it in a while, but this Thanksgiving will be special."

"*Ya*, I know the one." Catherine had made many recipes from her grandmother's cookbook. And again, this year, it would be a lot of work to prepare such a big meal for just the two of them. Catherine thought about all the leftovers they would eat for days, then freeze the rest. But her grandmother had looked regal during those Thanksgiving meals, always in a perfectly ironed dress, her gray hair meticulously swooped into a bun beneath her prayer covering, and she hadn't seemed bothered that it was only the two of them.

This year, Catherine found her grandmother's expectation of a large crowd odd. Would she be disappointed when no one showed up, or would she even remember that she was expecting a lot of people?

"And some folks will be coming early." Her grandmother grinned. "*Gott* told me that too."

Catherine wanted to get caught up in her grandmother's excitement, to dream that this vision could become a reality, to have even two other people to enjoy such a feast . . . but dreams led to disappointment. Catherine had allowed herself to wonder if anyone would invite them for Thanksgiving this year, but since it was only three days away, she supposed there would be no invites this year either. She suspected folks didn't want to tolerate her grandmother's antics, even though none of the outbursts or tall tales were her fault.

For today, it was good to see her grandmother in good spirits and excited. "I'll make sure everything is perfect," she said as she leaned over and kissed her on the forehead.

As she stood to leave, there was a knock at the front door, and her grandmother gasped.

"Our first visitors are here." She climbed out of bed. "I must get dressed." She waved both hands, palms up. "Go, now. Let them in, Jessica."

For what had seemed so normal quickly faded like a pin pricking a bubble, causing a loud pop in Catherine's ears.

But she took a deep breath and made her way to the front door.

CHAPTER 2

oah sighed as he waited for someone to open the door. "We don't even know these people," he said, hearing the frustration in his voice as he turned to Ruth.

"We don't really have a choice." She pulled her black snug around her when a burst of air swept beneath the porch rafters of the farmhouse. "The weather is supposed to be terrible, and the buses aren't expected to run tomorrow, possibly longer."

The wooden door slowly opened, and a young woman, perhaps Noah's age, mid-twenties, tentatively smiled. "*Wie bischt,*" she said softly. "Can I help you?"

"*Wie bischt,*" Noah said as his cheeks grew warm. The woman, with her light brown hair and emerald eyes was gorgeous. He was more embarrassed than he could have anticipated. After clearing his throat, he said, "We were booked to stay at The Peony Inn up the road . . ." He pointed over his shoulder.

"Well, we *thought* we were booked," Ruth interrupted, rolling her eyes as her teeth chattered.

"Please . . ." The woman eased open the screen door that separated them. "Come out of the cold."

Noah had been told by the owners of the inn that it was unseasonably cold for Montgomery, Indiana, which was causing them unexpected problems. Noah slowly crossed the threshold behind Ruth, carrying both of their suitcases. "*Danki*," he said as he set the luggage just inside the door before he and Ruth made their way to the fireplace, each warming their hands. Neither had gloves since they weren't expecting the icy mess.

The woman peered out the window before turning to face them. "Did you walk here?"

"It wasn't a far trek," Noah said, but that was before the wind had picked up and it began to drizzle snow.

"Anyway," Ruth said. "Our driver dropped us off at the place we were scheduled to stay. We thought we had booked a room at The Peony Inn for tonight, then had planned to travel the rest of the way to Missouri tomorrow where we are planning to have Thanksgiving with family. The owners of the inn, two elderly women, visited with us." Ruth put a finger to her chin. "I believe their names were Lizzie and Esther. They spoke with us for quite a while and even served us tea and lemonade before abruptly excusing themselves. When they returned, they said they didn't have a reservation on file for us, that they'd made a mistake." Ruth frowned, but quickly regrouped. "It didn't make much sense, but Lizzie, and her sister Esther, said you might have a room we could rent for the night."

Noah honed in on the beautiful woman, whose eyes were round as saucers now.

"We aren't a bed and breakfast. I'm so sorry. Lizzie and Esther should have sent you to another bed and breakfast in the area." She put a hand to her forehead. "I'm sorry," she said again.

"I knew this would happen," Noah said as he turned to Ruth, glaring at her. "We can't trust Hannah to do anything she says she'll do." He sighed before he looked at the woman again. "Our apologies for intruding on you this way. Do you know the closest bed and breakfast or inn within walking distance?"

CATHERINE GLANCED OUT THE WINDOW. It was beginning to snow harder. It was rare for Montgomery, Indiana, to have snow this time of year. How could she send these people out into the dismal weather? She was surprised that Lizzie and Esther had sent them her way, knowing what they did about her grandmother.

"Um . . ." She locked eyes with the man. "Please hang your coat and cape on the rack by the front door, then join me in the kitchen." She peeked out the window again. "It's snowing too hard to go anywhere just yet. I have hot *kaffi* or cocoa."

"*Danki*," the woman said as she left the warmth of the fire and slid out of her bonnet and cape. She also took off her shoes as did the man, who peeled off his coat and black knit cap.

Catherine scurried out of the den and into the kitchen,

which was toasty warm. She had a small propane heater going in the corner of the large room. Hastily, she slapped some day-old muffins, along with a loaf of banana nut bread she'd made that morning, onto a tray and placed it in the middle of the kitchen table.

"*Kaffi* or cocoa?" she asked as the couple entered the kitchen and took a seat.

"*Kaffi*," they both said in unison. "*Danki* again."

Catherine was busily scanning her mind for a solution to this dilemma as she poured coffee into the cups, facing away from them at her kitchen counter. They couldn't stay. What if her grandmother roamed the house without any clothes on? Unlikely, in this weather, but possible. Or she might just barge into the couple's room and sit on the edge of their bed. Catherine remembered how unnerved she felt the first time her grandmother had done that. She'd gotten used to it now.

She was placing a cup of coffee in front of each of them when her grandmother walked into the kitchen, fully dressed in a maroon dress and black apron, sporting a pair of black loafers that Catherine had bought her over a year ago. Her grandmother had refused to wear them. Until now. Catherine wondered what other surprises were in store for her and their guests. She reminded herself that her grandmother couldn't help what was happening to her.

"*Wie bischt*," her grandmother said. "I'm Mary Marie Byler." She nodded to Catherine. "And this is *mei* grand-daughter, Catherine."

Catherine breathed in a huge sigh of relief. But she also knew that her grandmother was quite capable of dropping onto all fours and crying, or a host of other behaviors that these strangers wouldn't understand.

"I'm Noah, and this is Ruth." The man introduced himself and the woman who Catherine assumed must be his wife. "I'm sorry we came here. Lizzie said that you had plenty of room and often housed their overflow of tenants. *Mei* apologies again."

Catherine made a mental note not to focus too much on the man, who .was very attractive. Tall and muscular with dark hair, deep brown eyes, and a square jawline. She didn't want to be caught ogling him. The couple were newly married based on the amount of facial hair on Noah. Not much at all, almost as if he just hadn't shaved recently. Catherine was trying to dream up a polite excuse as to why they would need to leave as soon as the weather cleared. She would offer to drive them in her buggy, and she'd just have to bring her grandmother along. Surely, there were rooms for rent at another establishment.

"We absolutely have plenty of room." Her grandmother pressed her palms together as she smiled. "It's no trouble for you to stay here."

Catherine's jaw dropped, but she snapped it closed when she saw the man staring at her, clearly waiting for a verbal reaction.

"Uh, *nee* . . . we've imposed." He kept his eyes on Catherine, and she wished he wouldn't. It made it hard to look away.

"Nonsense." Her grandmother sat at the head of the table with the couple to her right. She nodded out the kitchen window. "This isn't fit weather for travel, and you

27

certainly can't walk anywhere. I'm surprised Lizzie and Esther had you walk here."

Catherine recalled thinking the same thing. She silently thanked God that her grandmother was herself. At least for the moment.

"We left three days ago from Paradise, Pennsylvania, traveling mostly by bus and sometimes taking a taxi to where we'd planned to spend the night. We are trying to get to our relative's home in Missouri for Thanksgiving," Ruth said. "They live north of Jamesport."

Catherine's grandmother nodded, smiling. "I know that area. There is a large Amish community there. Although, I was very young when *mei* parents took me there." She scratched her chin, frowning. "I don't remember much about the trip."

"The forecast isn't very *gut* for your travels," Catherine said, flinching, as she wondered how she could have almost forced them into the weather. But would it be worse if the coyotes howled during the night as they often did during bad weather? It unnerved her grandmother and often sent her into a tailspin, worried about the animals surviving out in the elements.? Just the thought made her face feel like it was turning red. She didn't want to be embarrassed about her grandmother, the most giving and loving person she'd ever known. But her behavior was so unpredictable that Catherine was always on edge. Now, with guests in the house, it could be even worse.

"*Mei schweschder*, Hannah, said she made the reservations at The Peony Inn." Noah grinned, which caused a shiver to run up Catherine's spine, aware she shouldn't have such a reaction to a married man, especially just based upon his appearance. "She isn't always the most reliable person."

Ruth chuckled. "That's an understatement."

Catherine smiled. The woman was equally as pretty as her husband was handsome. She had the same dark hair, brown eyes, although with less of a square jawline.

"Well, *ach*, it's settled." Her grandmother smiled broadly at Noah, flashing a set of pearly white dentures that she rarely wore. "You and your *fraa* will be our guests until the weather is fit for travel."

Noah and Ruth looked at each other before they burst out laughing.

"*Fraa?*" Noah said before he chuckled again. "Ruth isn't *mei fraa*. She is *mei schweschder*."

Catherine gulped, her eyes now fixated on the handsome man across the table from her. She was at a loss for words. But when she finally looked back and forth between their guests, she could see the resemblance.

Her grandmother laughed. "*Ach*, well . . . this all makes sense now."

It made sense to Catherine too. Lizzie and Esther were known matchmakers in the community. Darling women. But the minute they found out that a handsome man like Noah was unattached, they'd sent him her way.

"What makes sense?" Ruth asked as she glanced back and forth between Catherine and her grandmother.

Please Mammi, *don't say anything about matchmaking.* Catherine's grandmother had been her normal self, but sometimes even her normal self spoke out of turn or said something to embarrass Catherine.

"*Ach,* nothing, dear." Her grandmother waved a hand and chuckled. "Don't mind me. I'm just a bit wacky sometimes."

Noah and Ruth shook their heads. "I'm sure not," they said almost at the same time.

"Go ahead . . ." Her grandmother laughed. "Tell them, Jessica. I'm a bit off *mei* rocker."

Catherine opened her mouth to say something, but her grandmother clicked her tongue.

"No need to agree with me, dear." Then she tipped her head to one side and eyed Catherine like she had no idea who she was.

"I'll show you to your rooms so you can get settled." Catherine stood, and luckily Noah and Ruth did too. "We'll serve dinner around noon."

Glancing at the clock on the wall, she realized that was only a half hour from now. Maybe she could convince her grandmother to eat now, then have her nap before Catherine played hostess to their guests.

CHAPTER 3

*A*fter thanking Catherine, Noah carried his red suitcase upstairs to the first room on the left, as instructed by his hostess. Then he placed Ruth's suitcase in her designated room down the hallway.

After unpacking a few toiletries, he went to check on his sister.

"It's a lovely room," Ruth said as she opened her suitcase atop her bed. "How is your room?"

"It's fine," Noah said as he took a seat in the rocking chair in the corner. It was a nice room, like his, with a queen bed and quilted cover, small dresser, rack for hanging clothes, and a lantern on the bedside table.

He tilted his head to one side and cast a slanted look at this sister. "Did you catch Mary Marie calling her granddaughter Jessica? I thought her name was Catherine."

"Her name *is* Catherine. Maybe she has another granddaughter named Jessica, and it was a slip of the tongue."

"*Ya*, maybe." He kicked the rocking chair into motion with his foot as he scratched his cheek. "It didn't seem like

Catherine wanted us to stay here." He paused, deliberating. "Maybe she has a boyfriend who will be upset that we are spending the night?"

"Maybe. Or maybe not." His sister looked over her shoulder and winked at him. "She's very pretty, and she looks about our age."

Noah and Ruth were twins. And at twenty-seven years old, Noah was considered an eligible bachelor, while Ruth was practically viewed as an old maid. It didn't seem fair since Ruth was a strong and confident woman, but most men were intimidated by her quick wit and sharp tongue. He prayed that his sister would find the perfect soulmate who would treat her with the respect she deserved.

"*Ya*, she's pretty, but I don't think she cared for us much." He raised an eyebrow. "Or maybe it was just me she didn't seem to like."

Ruth sat down on her bed after she'd hung her dresses on a rack in the room. "It wasn't that she didn't care for us." She pressed her lips together and squinted her eyes as if deep in thought. "I think she was nervous."

Noah's sister had a knack for reading people, but he wasn't sure if she was correct. "I don't know."

"I do." Ruth straightened. "And when she found out that I wasn't your *fraa*, she couldn't take her eyes off of you."

Noah's insides warmed despite the chill in the upstairs bedroom. "It was hard not to stare at her too."

Ruth chuckled. "*Ach!* I think that's the first time I've seen your eyes light up about a woman. You've had plenty of young ladies practically throw themselves at you over the years, but this one seems to have caught your eye." His sister sighed. "Too bad she lives so far away."

Noah laughed. "I don't know anything about her. Just because she's pretty on the outside doesn't mean she's pretty on the inside. I've learned that the hard way over the years."

"Well, let's go get to know her better." She glanced at the clock on the wall. "It's noon, and I'm sure you're hungry. I know I am."

Noah followed his sister down the stairs where they were met with an eerie silence. No utensils clanking, plates being laid out . . . just quiet.

They walked into the kitchen and eyed a spilt jar of milk on the floor, the contents still pouring out onto the wooden floor. Luckily the glass container hadn't broken. Ruth reached for a roll of paper towels and began cleaning up the mess while Noah put what was left of the milk in the refrigerator, which was slightly ajar.

"What do you think happened?" Noah asked in a whisper as Ruth stuffed the wet paper towels in the trashcan.

"I don't know." It was an uncommon response for Ruth, who, at the very least, usually had a speculation about a situation, if not the answer. "Wait. Look." She pointed out the window. "Catherine needs help." She raced to the rack by the front door and snatched her black cape.

"*Nee*, stay here. I'll go." Noah eased her aside and slipped into his black coat as he made his way outside. Blizzardly snow flew sideways as he crossed the yard, rushing through his ears like a stream of ice water since he hadn't taken the time to put on his knit cap.

"What's going on?" he asked Catherine as he squatted down next to her in the snow where she was huddled over her grandmother who was lying down. Neither woman had on a coat. Noah wasted no time taking off his jacket and draping it around Catherine's shoulders while her grandmother spread her arms and legs far and wide.

"She's making snow angels." Catherine's bottom lip trembled as she gazed into his eyes with a look of terror. "I can't get her to come in the *haus*. She's going to freeze to death."

Noah made a split-second decision because he couldn't let this frail woman freeze out here. He scooped Catherine's grandmother into his arms easily enough, despite her kicking and thrashing. He began to spin in circles, hollering "Wheeee!" She threw her head back and laughed. Noah spun her around until they were up the porch steps, then inside the house where he gently eased her out of his arms.

"*Grandmammi*, let's get you out of those wet clothes," Catherine said shivering, still with Noah's coat draped over her shoulders. She turned to him. "I'm so sorry," she whispered. "I'll just need to take care of her, then I'll have dinner on the table." Her bottom lip trembled as she looked at Ruth. "I'm sorry," she mouthed again as she led her grandmother out of the room. Mary Marie dragged her bare feet across the wooden floor. She had to be frozen.

Ruth sighed. "That's why she didn't want visitors." His sister spoke with the authority he was used to. "Come on.

Let's get something on the table for lunch. That poor woman has her hands full."

Noah followed her into the kitchen. "There's a bowl of something on the counter," he said pointing to a white bowl with a spoon next to it."

Ruth leaned down and sniffed the contents. "Chicken salad. You find the bread, and I'll get the table set."

"*Ya*, okay." Noah located the bread on the far side of the counter, but just as he set it on the table, he heard crying. Loud sobs.

"*Mammi*, it's okay. There's no need to cry," Catherine said as she peeled her grandmother's sopping wet apron off, then lifted her dress over her head before wrapping her in the blanket that she kept folded at the bottom of her bed. She retrieved a green dress from the rack and began to lower it over her grandmother's head.

"Jessica! Stop babying me!" her grandmother said as she pushed Catherine away. "I'm a grown woman. I can change *mei* own clothes." She snatched the dress from Catherine and pulled it over her head.

Catherine took a deep breath. As much as she loved her grandmother, sometimes it took everything she had not to yell at her. She prayed constantly for tolerance and patience. But when her grandmother hollered at her, it was especially hard not to fire back. "My name is Catherine," she said between gritted teeth.

"I know that." Her grandmother faced off with her. "Why would you say that?"

Catherine silently reprimanded herself for letting the situation get the best of her. "I don't know." She shook her head. Sometimes it was all she knew to say.

After asking her grandmother if she'd like a nap before supper, Cathrine pulled back the covers on the bed. Once she was tucked in, Catherine leaned down and kissed her on the forehead. "I *lieb* you, *Mammi*."

"I *lieb* you, too . . ." The older woman's eyes glazed over as she stared at Catherine, presumably searching for her name. Catherine knew better than to correct her again, and when she cupped Catherine's cheek with one hand, and looked at her with so much love in her heart, Catherine choked back tears.

"I know your name is Catherine. I know you are *mei* granddaughter." She paused as a tear rolled down her cheek. "And I know what is happening to me."

It was at these moments when Catherine begged God not to take her grandmother away from her in this fashion, one brain cell at a time.

Catherine tiptoed out of the room after her grandmother rolled over and pulled the covers up around her neck. Catherine would make sure she ate something later. Right now, she had to deal with her uninvited guests. Although, she wasn't sure what she would have done if Noah hadn't come outside to help.

After she changed her own wet clothes, she shuffled through the living room, then entered the kitchen. She eyed the kitchen table, put a hand to her chest, then lowered her head and cried.

CHAPTER 4

"*S*omeone needs a hug," Ruth said as she wrapped her arms around Catherine, and Catherine succumbed to the invitation, crying on the stranger's shoulder. After a few seconds, she eased away.

"*Mei* apologies." She found her grandmother's hero standing by a fully set table, complete with glasses of tea poured for four people. The chicken salad was on the table, along with a loaf of bread Catherine had made a few days ago. She recalled a time when she used to bake bread every morning.

"There's no need to apologize," Ruth said matter-of-factly. "Dementia or Alzheimer's?"

"Dementia."

Ruth shook her head. "I've seen *mei* parents' friends go through this with family. Where are your parents? Are you handling this all on your own? What about siblings?"

Catherine was taken aback at her directness, and embarrassed about crying on Ruth's shoulder, but she'd never see these people again after they left.

"I'm afraid the situation with *mei* parents is a long story, and I don't have any siblings." Catherine paused and forced a smile. "*Danki* for setting out lunch. That was very kind of you." Then she turned to Noah who was standing in the far corner of the kitchen, leaning against the counter with his ankles crossed. "I-I don't know what I would have done if you hadn't helped," she said, wishing her bottom lip would stop trembling as she pressed a hand to her chest. "*Danki* from the bottom of *mei* heart."

He nodded as his face blushed before he walked to the chair at the head of the table and pulled it out. "There is no need for you to apologize. I was happy to help with your *grandmammi,* and you look exhausted." He smiled. "Beautiful, but tired. So, please sit. There is no need to serve us. We are uninvited guests and happy to have a roof over our head for the night."

Catherine slowly eased into the chair he'd pulled out for her, grateful for the soft and compassionate way he spoke to her. *Beautiful?* She couldn't remember the last time someone told her that.

After Ruth took a seat next to Catherine, Noah slid into a chair on the other side of her.

"*Mammi* is napping, so we don't need to wait for her." Catherine bowed her head.

Following silent prayer, Ruth was the first one to reach for two slices of bread, then she lathered on chicken salad. "You need some help, you know?" she said to Catherine. "It's unfortunate that things will only get worse with your *mammi.* You can't do it alone."

Catherine knew she was right, but the thought of disgracing her grandmother by bringing in help felt wrong. She'd been so upset earlier when Catherine tried to help her out of her wet clothes. Her grandmother would be horribly embarrassed if a stranger were to see her at her most vulnerable.

"*Ya*, I suppose." Catherine folded her hands in her lap, choosing to wait until the others had made their sandwiches, but Ruth surprised her by placing the sandwich she'd just prepared onto Catherine's plate. Catherine raised an eyebrow and opened her mouth to speak.

"*Nee, nee*. No arguments. I know how easy it is not to eat when you are under duress, but you must keep up your strength." She smiled warmly before she reached for more bread for herself. Noah waited until his sister made her sandwich before preparing one for himself..

Catherine swallowed back a lump in her throat. She also couldn't recall the last time she'd felt nurtured. Ruth's confidence and nurturing ability shown through in her words and actions. She would make a great mother someday, Catherine thought as she nibbled on a corner of her sandwich. And Noah hadn't hesitated when he lifted Catherine's grandmother out of the snow and carried her inside.

It might only be for one night, but she was pleased that God had sent her these two unexpected guests. And credit also went to Esther and Lizzie, however misdirected their intentions might be. Catherine couldn't become romantically involved with anyone, especially someone who lived so far away. What were the sisters thinking? Catherine hoped Esther and Lizzie remembered to ask forgiveness for the lies they sometimes told in their matchmaking efforts. Catherine had questioned their antics years ago while she watched them trying to set up a couple. Lizzie had said they had God's blessing and that was all that mattered. Catherine wasn't sure about that, but she loved the two elderly women. It was hard to fault anyone who believed in romantic love as much as Esther and Lizzie.

"Sometimes, *mei mammi* is perfectly normal, and I treasure those times, when she knows who I am and is comfortable in her surroundings." She glanced back and forth between Noah and Ruth. "But her displays can be so outrageous that we don't get out much." She paused, sighing. "I'm not sure if that's such a *gut* thing. It gets lonely, but most of the time, when we've ventured out, it hasn't gone well."

Ruth was nodding as she took a sip of tea before saying, "I understand." After a long pause, she said, "Who is Jessica?"

Catherine shrugged. "I have no idea. She calls me by that name as often as she calls me Catherine."

"Hmm . . ." Ruth said before she glanced at her brother and chuckled. "Hungry, Noah?"

He covered his mouth with his hand as he chewed, then dabbed at his mouth with his napkin. Catherine had seen him make a second sandwich. "This is the best chicken salad I have ever had."

Pride was forbidden, but Catherine swelled with it just the same. *Another compliment.* "*Danki,*" she said with her eyes lowered on her plate, where she'd barely eaten anything. It seemed as if every nerve was always on edge, slowly coming unstitched like a sewing project she'd never finish. Her grandmother could come running into the room naked any minute, or possibly wearing her grandfather's clothes that she'd never discarded. Both had happened in the past.

Catherine finally looked up and studied Noah and Ruth. They looked almost identical except for the shadow of Noah's beard, and Ruth's smoother jawline, both of which she'd noticed before when she thought they were married. "Are you twins?" she asked.

"*Ya*, but I'm the oldest." Ruth chuckled again. "By six minutes. Noah couldn't decide if he wanted to join me out in the world."

Catherine laughed as she watched Noah smile. She liked these two people, who were feeling less and less like strangers. She glanced out the window. "The snow doesn't seem to be letting up. I wish we had access to a weather forecast."

Ruth wiped her mouth with her napkin before she reached into the pocket of her black apron and held up a mobile phone. "Let's check the forecast."

Catherine had a phone for emergencies, which most of their people did these days, but the bishop didn't allow phones with access to the Internet. Maybe Pennsylvania was more progressive. "Is that allowed?" Catherine spoke softly, hoping she wouldn't offend Ruth.

"*Nee*. It's not allowed in Pennsylvania, but I'm not there now." She winked at Catherine before she lowered her head and began to type. "Hmm . . . the weather isn't supposed to let up for days." She looked up at Noah. "We need to find somewhere to stay. And ugh, we might miss Thanksgiving with Fannie and Amos and their family."

"You're welcome to stay here as long as you'd like." Catherine felt badly that the weather might keep them from seeing their family on the holiday, but she found a sense of newfound hope at the possibility she could have guests for Thanksgiving.

Ruth shook her head. "We appreciate your offer to let us stay tonight, but we are an imposition, I know. We will find somewhere else nearby if we are unable to travel tomorrow." She continued to push buttons on her phone, and Catherine wondered if she was searching for bed and breakfasts in the area.

"Of course," Catherine said, hearing the tremble in her voice. "After what happened earlier, I'm sure you'd rather stay somewhere else."

Ruth slipped her phone back into her apron pocket. "Honey, what happened out in the yard isn't our reason for not staying." She paused, glancing at her brother before she went on. "We don't want to cause you any additional stress."

Normally, Catherine would find it odd that someone her age would call her 'honey', but it seemed so natural for Ruth. And genuine.

Catherine chose to side with the truth. "I know it probably seemed that way when you first arrived. I was afraid *mei mammi* would do something like she did this morning, and I didn't want anyone to see that. But . . ." She smiled. ". . . now that I've gotten to know you, if only a little bit, I'm enjoying your company."

Ruth put her elbows on the table and cupped her chin in her hands. "*Ach*, well . . . if the weather doesn't clear, we might be stuck here. And by stuck here, I don't mean that in an unpleasant way. Just that we might not make it to see our family by Thanksgiving. But *Gott* has a way of taking a bad situation and turning it to *gut*. So, we will stay if you are sure it's all right, if it comes to that."

"I would like that, unless the weather clears, and I know you will want to be with your family."

Ruth grinned at her brother. "You're awfully quiet, *bruder*."

He shrugged, then chuckled. "You don't leave much room for anyone else to talk."

Catherine covered her mouth with her hand to hide her smile.

"*Ach*, because most of what I have to say is important. You ramble." Ruth laughed, but it was such good-natured bantering that Catherine finally laughed aloud as well.

It was a nice moment that ended too soon when Catherine's grandmother yelled. "Jessica?"

Catherine stood, but so did Ruth. "Let me see if I can tend to her," Ruth said.

"*Ach*, I don't know if you want to do that. She can get . . . physical when she gets really confused."

Catherine kept standing until Ruth put a hand on her shoulder. "She'll be fine. I'll be fine."

Catherine lowered herself back on the chair, and after Ruth had passed through the living room and was out of earshot, she said, "She doesn't usually take no for an answer, does she?" Catherine followed up the comment with a smile so that Noah could see the appreciation in her expression.

He laughed. "*Usually?* I'd say more like never."

"You two are close, *ya*?" Catherine had always heard that twins have a special bond.

He gazed into Catherine's eyes. "Ruth is great. I'm blessed to call her *mei schweschder*."

"She's so strong, confident, and beautiful. Is she married?" Catherine was surprised the subject hadn't come up.

Noah smiled. "*Nee*, she's not married. And courtship is one thing she can say *nee* about. She's had plenty of suitors, but so far, no one has been able to hold her attention. And she can be a little scary until you get to see the beauty she has stored up inside."

"It's nice, the way you talk about your *schweschder*. I always wanted *bruders* and *schweschdere*, but it just wasn't in *Gott's* plan." She shrugged. "Is Hannah your only other sibling?"

"*Nee*, there are nine of us, but Ruth and I are the oldest. *Mamm* and *Daed* agreed to let us travel to Missouri for Thanksgiving because *mei* aunt was really putting pressure on *mei* parents to visit them, and there are just so many of us." He laughed. "I think our relatives were hoping our parents would go. Ruth and I are their consolation prize, I guess you could say." After chuckling, he said, "And I'm the only *sohn*."

Catherine raised her eyebrows. "*Ach*, really?" He nodded. "I'm sorry that it might not work out, you arriving there in time for Thanksgiving."

Noah smiled again. "Do you have a turkey? I thought I saw one at the back of the refrigerator when I put what was left of the bottle of milk inside."

She stared at him, a gleaming hint of interest in his eyes, which locked with hers. She wasn;t going to think about that spilt milk earlier. "Um, *ya*, I do."

"Then everything will be just fine." Noah winked at her.

She felt the meaning in the gesture like Cupid's arrow straight into her heart. But eventually, the weather would clear, and life would go back to the way it was.

"It sounds like Ruth has things under control in the other room. I'd like to help you clear the table, and—"

"*Nee, nee.*" Catherine quickly stood. "I can't have you do that. You've already done so much."

He picked up his and his sister's plates and carried them to the sink before he turned to her. "Then why don't I go add some logs to the fire, and if all is well with your *mammi*, maybe we could all participate in afternoon devotion? Despite the circumstances, we have a lot to be thankful for."

"You're right," she said as she walked to the kitchen counter where he was standing. "I'll meet you in the living room shortly."

He winked at her again before he left, and this time, she felt the breath drain from her lungs. It was an uncomfortable and wonderful feeling wrapped into an adventure she wouldn't get to have.

CHAPTER 5

*N*oah added two logs to the fire, stoked it until orange embers wafted upward, then sighed.

"You just met her," Ruth said in a whisper as she rounded the corner from the hallway. "But you're already smitten with her. I can see it all over your face. You even told her she was beautiful." She patted him on the back as she shuffled toward the couch. "*Gut* for you, *bruder*."

Noah had surprised himself with the admission about Catherine. "*Ya*, she is very pretty, and I feel badly for her, being alone and dealing with her *mammi*."

Ruth sat on the couch and slouched into the cushion as she folded her arms across her chest. "Interesting. I've not seen you react this way toward a woman."

"You've already said that." He shrugged before he sat down beside his sister. "And she lives a million miles away from us."

Ruth nudged him with her elbow. "Not exactly a *million* miles, but we are pretty far from Pennsylvania." She sighed. "Just enjoy your time here. We never know what the Lord has in store for us. I think we will end up having Thanksgiving with our new friends." She shook her head. "Unless the forecast changes drastically, we're going to be here through Thanksgiving. And, if that happens, I want us to make it really special for Catherine and her *mammi*." She paused. "Fannie and her family will be disappointed if that happens, but I feel strongly that God has sent us here for a reason."

Noah nodded. "*Ya*, I agree with all of that. And if we're here for Thanksgiving, we can at least make it special for Catherine and Mary Marie, to repay Catherine's hospitality." He was starting to hope the weather didn't clear. He rubbed his chin. "Actually, we should probably offer to pay her."

Ruth cringed. "*Ya*, you're right. Where are our manners?"

Catherine walked into the room and folded her hands in front of her. "Noah suggested that we have devotions together. Is that okay with you, Ruth?"

"*Ya, ya*," Ruth said before she tapped a finger to her chin. "Also, we were just discussing how we would like to pay you for whatever time we stay here."

Catherine shook her head right away. "*Nee, nee*. I have plenty of food and room. I only hesitated in the beginning for fear of *Mammi's* behavior. But you've seen that." She looked down, her long lashes brushing against flushed cheeks.

Noah wanted to hug her, but he couldn't stand up from the couch and rush to her. Although, he had an overwhelming desire to do so. "We aren't worried about your *mammi*, about what she may or may not do. So, please don't upset yourself."

"*Danki*," she said before she glanced over her shoulder. "I'm going to go take a peek at *Mammi* and make sure she's all right." She smiled before she left the room, and Noah couldn't take his eyes off her.

"Wow." Ruth rolled her eyes. "You've got it bad for her."

Noah grinned. "I know. And it's not just because she's gorgeous." He thought about his response. "She's so nice . . . so kind . . . and . . ."

"I think sweet is the word you are looking for," Ruth said in a whisper when she heard Catherine's footsteps.

"She's still sleeping," Catherine said as she walked back into the room. "That was a lot of excitement for her earlier. I'll try to get her to eat something later."

Ruth yawned. "*Ach, mei*. I'm sleepy after that delicious meal. I think I'm going to skip devotions this afternoon. I'll make it up to *Gott* this evening." She covered her mouth as she yawned again. "I'm going to take a nap if that's okay with you, Catherine?"

"Of course." She glanced at Noah, who grinned at his sister before she walked out of the room. He knew what she was up to. And he loved her for it.

He cleared his throat as his eyes shifted to Catherine, still standing in the middle of the living room. "If you're tired also . . ."

"*Nee*," she responded quickly. "Um, but if you are—"

He shook his head. "*Nee*." He nodded to the spot on the couch next to him where his sister had been. "I'd be happy to pray with you."

Catherine hesitated as she walked slowly toward him and sat down, leaving a foot between them on the couch before she reached for her Bible on the coffee table.

"I must confess," she said as her eyes averted his. "I haven't been as *gut* about daily devotions as I should be. *Mammi* usually gets bored or confused before we are finished. We missed this morning." She smiled sweetly. "I *lieb* praying with someone else, so *danki* for suggesting it. Where would you like to begin?" She laid her hands atop the Bible.

Noah thought for a few moments. "Why don't we get to know each other better, then perhaps *Gott* will lead us in the direction He intends for us?"

"I like that idea." She smiled again. "You go first. Tell me about yourself." She twisted to face him, her skirt fanning out over her legs as she tucked one foot beneath her with inquiring eyes.

"Hmm . . ." He rubbed his stubbly chin. "Let's see. I already told you that me and Ruth are part of a large family with nine of us *kinner*. We live just outside of Paradise, a city in Lancaster County, Pennsylvania. It's getting more and more touristy in the city, but that lends itself to a *gut* income, so I reckon it's a trade-off. I do construction work with *mei daed*, and *mei schweschdere* run a boutique where they sell handmade items, like kitchen towels, potholders with potpourri, cookbooks, and faceless dolls. *Mei mamm* mostly takes care of the *haus* and meals." He paused with a shrug. "We aren't wealthy or proud, but we make a decent living."

Catherine nodded. "I'm not afraid of hard work, but I'm grateful I don't have to struggle to make money, which would be a difficult task under the circumstances. *Mei* grandfather owned a successful welding business when he was alive and left *mei mammi* in a good financial position. But I plant a plentiful garden in the spring and colorful blooms in the flowerbeds." She raised one shoulder before lowering it slowly. "I keep things running as best I can."

"It's a lot for one person to take on, but you seem to handle it with grace." He smiled, thinking Ruth was right. He was becoming smitten with this woman.

"*Danki*," she said as she looked down, then raised her eyes to his. "It must be very different for you here. I mean, you haven't seen much of our small community, but we are . . ." She giggled for the first time, and it was cute, causing him to smile. ". . . small. Very small. Our total population is around eight hundred people, including the *Englisch*. Our district has about two hundred members, but there are others nearby." She looked over her shoulder and out the window. "This is so uncommon for us to have this kind of snow in November, close to Thanksgiving. I can only recall one other time we had enough snow to keep people practically homebound during the holiday week."

Noah glanced out the window. "You don't have any neighbors. At home, we have a lot of acreage, but we can still see neighbors. I like the privacy here."

She twirled the string of her prayer covering, looking down again. "A little too private sometimes. As I said before, I don't get out much because of *Mammi*."

"You're a *gut* granddaughter to care for her the way you do." Noah believed that the elderly should be given extra care, especially if they have declining health. "I bet she has a lot of stories to tell. How old is she?"

"Seventy-eight. Her dementia started about four years ago, slowly at first. She'd forget little things, put items where they didn't belong, and things like that. It has gotten especially bad over the past year."

Noah frowned. "Where I live, people pitch in and help with a situation like this."

"*Ach*, plenty offered at first, but I have turned down people so many times that they quit asking. Folks visit, but it's never for long." She sighed. "*Mammi* is a proud woman, whether that fits with our beliefs or not. She is dignified, and as she approaches her final years, I want her to feel that she hasn't lost that dignity. Bringing in outside help would steal her sense of self-worth, I think."

"Is that why you're not married?" He cringed at the directness of his question. "I'm sorry That's not *mei* business."

She chewed on her bottom lip. "*Nee*, it's okay. I just don't have much of a social life. *Mammi* takes up most of *mei* time." She slid her gaze his way. "I guess I'm an old maid."

Noah laughed. "I'm sorry, but you aren't old, and you're definitely not an old maid. You're very beautiful. And kind." He felt his face begin to flush. "I hope that's not too forward, but with everything you do for your *mammi,* you deserve a genuine compliment."

CATHERINE WAS BASKING in the company of such a handsome man who gave compliments so freely. But he had yet to ask her the one question that would lead him to question her family structure. She often wondered if some of her situations were hereditary. "You haven't asked *mei* about *mei* parents."

"You said when we first met that it was complicated. Don't feel you have to explain if you're not comfortable doing so."

Catherine stared at him. She couldn't help it. There was such sincerity in his words, but she wanted to get it over with. "*Mei* parents left the community and got an *Englisch* divorce. Of course, they were shunned, so I can't see them. I do exchange letters with *mei mamm*, but I don't hear from *mei daed*. *Mammi* is *mei* maternal *grandmammi*." She chuckled, but it wasn't real, more of a disgruntled half-laugh that escaped somehow. "So, I come from a dysfunctional and unhealthy family. I'm not really marriage material."

She held her breath, already wishing she hadn't shared so much. She could have at least spent time in a fantasy world with Noah until he left soon.

He twisted to face her, their knees touching in the space between them. "I think you're everything a *fraa* should be. You are not a reflection of your parents, and the way you tend to your *mammi* is admirable. You have a kind heart, which is something to be cherished in any relationship."

Catherine wanted to jump into his arms, if for nothing more than a hug. She longed the feel of physical closeness. Her grandmother wasn't very affectionate most of the time, and she didn't realize how starved she was for the warmness of human touch. "I appreciate that very much." She wanted to veer things away from herself.

"What about you though?"

Still facing her, with his knee resting against hers, he propped his elbow on the back of the couch and rested his head against his hand. "I told you, we run a construction company, and—"

"Why aren't you married?" She pressed her lips together, cringed, and said, "Too personal?"

"*Nee*. I asked you the same thing." He grinned. "The difference is that if I tell you, you will think less of me, for sure."

Catherine grinned back at him, intrigued. "Well, now you *have* to tell me."

He sighed as he lowered his arm and shook his head. "I warned you."

"I consider myself warned." She gave a taut nod of her head. "Now, tell me these awful things that will make me think less of you." She couldn't imagine.

"I've been in two serious courtships, and both women were on a fast track toward marriage. One of them was perfect for me in every way. We enjoyed the same interests, thought about things the same, but I just wasn't physically attracted to her enough to spend the rest of *mei* life with her. I'm sure that sounds vain."

"*Nee*, I don't think that's vain." She waited for more, but when he didn't offer up any additional information, she asked, "And the other relationship?"

"Awe." He closed his eyes and leaned his head back. "If

I tell you about the other one, you'll see me for the scoundrel I really am."

Catherine laughed, which brought forth a swirl of anticipation, no matter what sort of confession Noah was about to lay out in front of her, to bear witness to the type of person he was. She already thought he was wonderful. "All right, you scoundrel, let's hear it."

He squeezed his eyes closed, took a deep breath, then took an exaggerated look around the room as if to make sure no one could hear. "She couldn't cook."

Catherine burst out laughing. "I know you are teasing!" She hadn't meant to speak so loudly, but it was an outrageous comment. "All Amish women know how to cook. We are taught very young. Some might be better than others, but I'm sure your intended could cook."

"*Nee*, she couldn't," he said with an exaggerated frown on his face. "I'm being truthful."

"And that's the only reason you chose not to marry this woman?" Catherine couldn't stop grinning. Because she didn't believe him.

"What can I say? I like to eat." He frowned. "I told you that you would think less of me."

Catherine playfully slapped him on the arm, then left her hand resting on the couch, less than an inch away from his shoulder. "You're teasing."

He reached up and caressed the top of her hand. "*Ya*, I am. It's true that she wasn't a very *gut* cook, but she also wasn't the right woman for me."

Catherine's eyes drifted to his hand on hers as a welcomed warmth crept into her like a lost blanket of companionship that she didn't know she needed.

She wanted to be in his arms, and she allowed herself to fantasize about him kissing her, but he jerked his hand away when they heard footsteps descending the stairs.

Ruth reached the landing, put her hands on her hips, and clicked her tongue. "Tsk, tsk. I don't hear any devotions going on in here, just a lot of laughing."

Catherine covered her mouth with her hand to keep Ruth from seeing the smile spread across her face.

Ruth frowned, but in a playful way. "I'm surprised you haven't woken up your *mammi*." She yawned. "You didn't bother me. I just couldn't sleep."

A knock at the door jarred them all.

Catherine glanced out the window, surprised to see a buggy hitched to the fence, then she sprung up and moved quickly toward the door. On the other side was a man about her age. A very tall and handsome fellow that she'd never seen before. She swallowed hard when her eyes landed on the suitcase he was holding in one hand.

CHAPTER 6

*N*oah couldn't help but notice the man's well-built physique, broad shoulders, and dazzling blue eyes. Had his competition for Catherine's affections just entered the room? He hadn't realized there was a contest in play until just now. He stood and waited for an introduction, but Catherine didn't seem to know this man.

"Lizzie and Esther did what?" she asked, looking taken aback and surprised as she pushed the screen door open and asked him to come in out of the cold. It was almost an exact replica of the earlier scene when Noah and Ruth had arrived. Except this man was alone.

The visitor set his suitcase just inside the door, the same way Noah had done with his and Ruth's luggage. "They said there was no room at the inn, to quote them exactly," the Amish man said in a deep voice with a concerned look on his face. "Am I mistaken to assume you have a room for me, as they said?"

Catherine glanced at Noah, who merely shrugged.

BETH WISEMAN

Then they both looked at Ruth, whose mouth hung open. Noah wasn't sure he'd ever seen his sister at a loss for words, as she seemed to be now.

"I would need to stay until the storm clears," the man said. "I'm on *mei* way home, to Orleans, but *mei* horse can't make it in this weather." He shook his head. "I've never seen it so snowy this time of year."

Catherine put a hand to her forehead as she leaned to her left to see out the window. She knew where Orleans was, and the man was right. By car it would only be forty-five minutes, but much longer for a horse, and certainly not doable in this weather.

"We aren't exactly a bed and breakfast," she said. "But we seem to be taking some of The Peony Inn's overflow." She pointed out the window. "There is an empty stall in the barn if you'd like to shelter your horse from the weather." She extended her hand. "I'm Catherine Lapp." A few seconds later, she nodded to Ruth, then to Noah. "These are guests who also had reservations at The Peony Inn. That's Ruth and her *bruder*, Noah."

Noah stepped forward and shook the man's hand, cutting his eyes at his sister, who had managed to close her mouth, but hadn't moved or spoken. "I'll help you get your horse settled in the barn," Noah said as he speculated about his sister's behavior. Since Noah had noticed the man's handsome features, Ruth probably had also. But it wasn't her style to clam up this way.

"I'd be grateful. *Mei* name is Leroy Stoltzfus."

Noah acknowledged the introduction with a nod, then took his coat from the rack and slipped into his black boots before covering his head with his black knit cap. "We'll be back."

He had been hoping to have more alone time with Catherine, but that seemed unlikely now.

CATHERINE WAS TRYING to decide if this was an emergency and whether the addition of another uninvited guest justified calling the owners of The Peony Inn. She found it hard to believe that Lizzie and Esther had overbooked rooms.

"I heard men's voices."

Her grandmother came into the room fully clothed in the dark green dress she'd changed into earlier. It was wrinkled, but that was okay. She also had her hair in a bun and tucked beneath her prayer covering.

"*Ya, Mammi.* Apparently, Lizzie and Esther sent someone else here after telling the man that they were full."

"*Ach*, well, the more the merrier." Her grandmother shrugged.. "I'm hungry."

"We ate chicken salad earlier. Would you like for me to make you a sandwich?"

"Why in the world would you eat without me? We always eat together." She glanced at Ruth who hadn't moved or spoken. "Did you get something to eat, Ruth?"

Ruth nodded.

Catherine was glad that her grandmother remembered their new house guest and grateful that she didn't seem to recall making snow angels in the freezing weather earlier.

"I'll go make a sandwich and leave you two *maeds* to chat." Her grandmother shuffled in her black socks across the living room toward the kitchen.

Ruth still hadn't spoken or moved.

"Are you okay?" Catherine asked her.

"Um . . . *ya.*" Ruth blinked her eyes a few times before she moved to the couch, sat, and looked over her shoulder out the window.

"Are you sure you are all right?" Catherine moved slowly closer to her, putting a hand on her arm. She could see Noah and Leroy out the window, guiding the horse into the barn.

"What?" Ruth blinked her eyes a few times. "I'm sorry. Did you say something?"

"I was just making sure you're okay." Catherine was wondering if this day could get any more bizarre. She'd been praying for companionship, for help with her grandmother, and to not feel so lonely most of the time. God had heard her loud and clear. Her house was filling up faster than she ever thought possible. She recalled what her grandmother had said about having a crowd for Thanksgiving. Could God have really told her such a thing?

"Of course. Of course." Ruth stood and smoothed the wrinkles from her black apron as she smiled. "*Ya.* I'm fine."

Catherine needed to call Esther and Lizzie. Her predicament might not constitute an emergency, but she wouldn't have any spare bedrooms left if the sisters tried to send anyone else her way.

"Ruth, can you keep an eye on *mei mammi?* I need to

make a phone call." She paused. "I'm not sure why Esther and Lizzie are sending people here to stay. I mean, it's perfectly fine that you and Noah are here. And I suppose it's all right that Leroy is here too. But I'm out of spare rooms now."

"*Ya*, I need a drink anyway." Ruth blew loose strands of hair out of her face before she left the room. Catherine hoped that tea, coffee, or milk would suffice because they didn't drink alcohol in her district, except maybe at a wedding. Ruth had made the comment as if she might want something stronger than what Catherine kept on hand.

She entered her bedroom and closed door, then took her cell phone from her nightstand, deciding this could be a mini emergency. She called The Peony Inn and recognized Lizzie's voice when she answered.

"Lizzie, it's Catherine Lapp." They had six Catherines in her district. "I wanted to let you know that *mei* extra bedrooms are all full now. Did you accidentally overbook?"

"I'm sharp as a tack, and I'd never do that." Lizzie huffed.

"Could Esther have made the error?"

Lizzie chuckled. "Esther is sharper than I am on most days. But I know a perfect match when I see one. Isn't Noah the most handsome man you have ever seen? He was only inside for a short while, but when he said he wasn't married, I knew he was the man for you."

Catherine closed her eyes and shook her head. "Lizzie, how could you possibly know that? He is only passing through anyway." She knew the sisters were notorious matchmakers, but this was a stretch even for Lizzie and Esther.

"*Gott* told me to send Noah your way," Lizzie said. "And when *Gott* tells you to do something, you don't ignore it."

Catherine grinned. God was giving instructions to everyone around her, it seemed. But she did have a spark for Noah, and he seemed like he might have an interest in her. Although, it had nowhere to go. "Don't you think that's inappropriate to send an unmarried man to sleep under the same roof as I am?" She was doing her own stretching now.

"*Ach, nee.* You're not teenagers, and you have chaperones—his sister Ruth and your *grandmammi.*"

"Lizzie, I've told you and Esther both in the past that I am not in a position for romance. *Mammi* needs *mei* constant attention." For a few moments she allowed herself to imagine being with Noah, a man she didn't know but whom she seemed to have been waiting for all her life. If only Lizzie was being truthful by saying that God had told her to send Noah her way. Then she had a thought. "If you're so busy playing matchmaker between me and Noah, then why did you send Leroy here as well? Are they both supposed to be competing for *mei* attention?"

Lizzie laughed again. "Now, don't get greedy. They are both handsome fellows. But Leroy is for Ruth. When I interviewed—I mean talked to—Leroy . . ." She cleared her throat. "*Gott* whispered in *mei* ear that Leroy is perfect for Ruth."

Catherine rolled her eyes. Then she recalled the way

Ruth had turned to stone when Leroy arrived. God worked in mysterious ways, but this all seemed unlikely and geographically impossible. "Lizzie, Ruth and Noah live a very long way from here."

"Listen." Lizzie huffed, and Catherine could picture the tiny woman slamming her hand to her hip and shuffling her dentures around the way she was known to do. "The four of you are all twenty-seven years old. It makes sense. You're all beautiful people."

"Relationships aren't built on the age of a person." Catherine assumed Lizzie knew every single person's age in her district. "Did you get that information from Ruth and Noah while you were *interviewing* them?" She didn't know if Leroy had succumbed to the same type of interview, or if Lizzie was guessing about his age.

"Listen," Lizzie said again, sounding annoyed. "I'm sure your *mammi* doesn't want you to be an old maid. I'm sure Ruth's people don't want her to be one either. The men . . . well, folks are more understanding about an unmarried man who is late into his twenties. Everything will work out with your *mammi* too."

A flicker of hope sparked in Catherine's mind, but she'd been told that her grandmother's condition would only worsen. "*Mammi* isn't going to get better," she said in a trembling voice.

"Awe, hon. I know that," Lizzie said sweetly. "Just trust the Lord." She chuckled. "And trust me and Esther too. Now, I must go. Keep your heart open, dear one."

Catherine hit End on the phone when the line went dead, turned it off, and put it back in her nightstand. She sat on her bed with her hands folded in her lap. Why would God send her someone she might really like but whom she couldn't have? And why would God also send Leroy to Ruth from so many states away?

Then her grandmother screamed, and there was a loud noise in the kitchen. Ruth yelled, "Don't move!"

Catherine bolted from her bedroom.

CHAPTER 7

*C*atherine jogged through the living room and stopped cold when she reached the kitchen. Her grandmother was standing on a chair, and Ruth had a broom in her hand, trying to direct a mouse toward the opened door that led to the porch from the kitchen. Blustery winds sent in a swoosh of cold air as tiny flecks of snow dotted the wood floor.

"*Ach! Mammi*, get down!" Catherine was more concerned about her grandmother on top of a chair than she was about the mouse. She rushed to the chair, prepared to help the older woman down from the height, but her grandmother slapped her extended hand away.

"You know how I feel about rodents, Jessica!" She brought both hands to her chest, holding her position on the chair.

Catherine wasn't sure what to do as Ruth continued trying to swoosh the mouse toward the kitchen door that led outside.

"What's wrong?" Noah was breathless as he entered

the kitchen through the open door still with his hat and coat on. Leroy was behind him, also still in his winter jacket, both men speckled with white snowflakes against black coats.

"Mouse!" Catherine's grandmother screamed, pointing to Ruth who had given up the chase and stood perfectly still, her eyes wide. The mouse wasn't anywhere to be seen.

"First let's get you down off that chair." Noah lifted Catherine's grandmother with both hands around her waist and gently set her on the floor. "Your visitor is gone." He waved a hand around the room, then stopped briefly to look at his sister, who had turned to stone again.

"Excuse me," Ruth said before she blew hair from her face and left the room. "*Mammi*, are you okay?" Catherine glanced around the corner at Ruth in the living room. She was sitting on the couch with her head in her hands. "*Ya*. I'm fine." She shrugged, frowning. "I just don't like mice."

Catherine glanced at Ruth again, then turned to Leroy. "*Mei* apologies for the chaos. As I said, we aren't officially a bed and breakfast." She nodded to her grandmother and cleared her throat. "And there are reasons for that."

Leroy pointed over his shoulder toward the window. "Should I go?"

Catherine shook her head. "*Nee*, of course not. The weather is terrible." She grinned at him, shrugging. "As long as you don't mind a little disorder from time to time."

Leroy smiled. "*Nee*, not at all. Please let me know if you need help with anything and what I owe you for the room each night."

Catherine smiled back at him, taking note of the kindness in his voice. But she could also feel someone's eyes burning a hole through her. She turned to Noah, who frowned. Maybe he was concerned about his sister. They didn't know this man, and now he'd be staying overnight also.

"*Mammi*, are you all right now?" she asked as she looked away from Noah.

Her grandmother shrugged. "*Nee*. I will not be okay until that mouse has been relocated."

For a woman who had chopped off the heads of chickens for as long as Catherine could remember, she was uncharacteristically afraid of mice. Her grandmother had wrangled with snakes, delivered calves, and taken on a coyote with only a stick in her hand.

Catherine closed the kitchen door. "He's probably moved on, *Mammi*, and scooted outside." She leaned her head far to the right until she could see Ruth sitting on the couch with her head still in her hands. "I'm going to go check on Ruth." She glanced back and forth between Noah and Leroy, both nice-looking men, but Noah was handsome in a way that warmed Catherine all the way to her core. It was more than just a physical attraction, and she reminded herself that a long-distance relationship was nothing that could ever be.

"Please help yourself to *kaffi* and any snacks on the table." She waved a hand over a tray filled with sticky buns, cookies, and other treats she'd set out earlier.

Ruth lifted her head when Catherine walked into the living room. The woman's face was flushed, and her hands trembled in her lap.

"*Ach, mei.*" Catherine sat beside her on the couch. "I'm so sorry you had to deal with that mouse. You must be as frightened of those critters as *mei mammi.*"

Ruth scowled. "I'm not afraid of a little mouse." She stiffened as she sat taller. "It's . . ." She raised her chin as she huffed. "It's that man."

"What man? Leroy?" Catherine asked as she tipped her head to one side.

"He unnerves me in a way that I can't explain." She put a hand on Catherine's. "Forgive me if I sounded curt." She sighed. "I don't know what's gotten into me." Then she seemed to force a smile. "Silliness, really." Then she groaned. Her expressions and emotions were shifting faster than Catherine could keep up. "I don't know what I'm saying, and that is so unlike me, to freeze up around a man I don't even know. My insides fill with butterflies when he is around."

Catherine stifled a smile as she began to understand Ruth's reaction to Leroy. She twisted to face her. "I talked to Lizzie on the phone, the woman you met briefly at The Peony Inn." She grinned. "She sent Leroy here for you. Lizzie and her sister love to play matchmakers, and they pride themselves by believing they always pick suitable candidates for courting."

"That's . . ." Ruth hesitated but chuckled. "Nonsense."

"There's more." Catherine snickered. "Lizzie and Esther believe that your *bruder* is a *gut* match for me. They probably have plenty of rooms at the inn. They are just doing what they do, playing matchmakers."

Ruth raised an eyebrow. "I don't know about Leroy,

but I've noticed the way *mei bruder* looks at you. I don't believe I've ever seen him look at someone that way."

Catherine felt herself blushing. "Your *bruder* is a handsome man, but I'm not in the market for courtship." She lowered her head and stared at her hands folded in her lap. "I must take care of *mei mammi*, and sometimes it's a full-time job. I don't mind though. I *lieb* her very much." Part of it was a tiny lie. Catherine often envisioned herself in the arms of a man, someone like Noah, and she often wished things could be different. But her grandmother came first.

"*Mei bruder* is a *gut* man," Ruth said as she locked eyes with Catherine. "And perhaps your matchmaking friends, Lizzie and Esther, did a *gut* thing by sending us here."

Catherine grinned. "Do you want to hear something shocking?"

Ruth chewed on her bottom lip, also grinning slightly. "*Ya*, sure."

"I heard, from a very *gut* source, that one time Lizzie slipped a, um . . . love potion into a couple's drink, convinced it would make them fall in *lieb*."

Ruth bent at the waist and buckled in laughter. "You don't believe that do you?"

Catherine shrugged. "I don't know. The couple ended up getting married."

Ruth stopped laughing. "Hmm." Then she shook her head. "I don't believe in such things."

"I really don't either, but it's a cute story, although initially, the *maed* involved had a reaction to Lizzie's potion. But all ended up well."

Catherine thought for a few moments, feeling more

comfortable sharing with Ruth. "Even if Noah and I hit it off, there is the geography issue, in addition to *mei* . . . living situation."

Ruth shrugged. "Sometimes, *Gott* has a plan we can't foresee."

Catherine nudged Ruth's shoulder. "That could apply to you and Leroy as well."

Ruth quickly shook her head. "*Nee, nee* . . . I could never get involved with a man who makes *mei* stomach flip the way he does."

"But is it in a *gut* way or a bad way?"

Ruth raised her eyebrows. "I don't even know him. And I don't want to get to know him." She stood. "Please let the others know I'm going to go lay down, but I will be downstairs in plenty of time to help you prepare supper."

Catherine didn't say anything as she watched Ruth go upstairs. She wondered if maybe no one had ever shaken the confident, poised Ruth the way Leroy's presence did. It would be interesting to watch it play out. Ruth was smitten with Leroy whether she realized it or not. But even as she sat pondering about Ruth and Leroy, visions of her and Noah crept into her mind, drowning in regret that she'd never know if romance could have been in her future with him.

Noah busied himself on the couch, pretending to read a book, when all he wanted to do was go into the kitchen and be near Catherine. He wondered if Leroy was having those same thoughts about Catherine—or his sister—as he sat in the rocking chair across from Noah with a gardening magazine in his hands. He also wondered whether Leroy had overheard the conversation between Catherine and Ruth, the way he had—and, if not, should Noah share what he heard? He couldn't stop thinking about what he'd heard Catherine say--*Your* bruder *is a handsome man, but I'm not in the market for courtship.* Noah knew that their situation didn't bide well for romance, but she thought he was handsome, and that was enough to consume his thoughts.

After a few moments, Leroy cleared his throat. "So, where do your travels take you once you leave here?"

Noah looked up. "We began in Lancaster County, Pennsylvania. We were on our way to spend Thanksgiving with relatives in Missouri, and we had a scheduled stop at The Peony Inn."

Pots and pans banged around in the kitchen where Catherine and her mother were.

"I had a reservation as well." Leroy rubbed his chin. "Seems odd that they'd overbook."

"But did they?" Noah grinned, deciding he would share what he'd overheard even though he had his guard up about Leroy.

"What do you mean?"

Noah told Leroy everything he'd heard Catherine and Ruth talking about, and Leroy smiled the entire time. "Really?" he finally said before he chuckled. "I don't believe in magic potions, but the sisters' tactics make sense now. When I entered the *haus*, they asked me if I was married, if I was traveling alone, where I was headed . . ." He smiled broader. "After I'd answered all their questions, they told me they were completely booked and I needed to make other arrangements, that they were happy to take care of it. It was like . . ."

"An interview," Noah said before chuckling. "They did the same thing with me and Ruth, now that I think about it."

"Is—um . . . your *schweschder* married or spoken for?" Leroy looked down at the magazine as he posed the question. "I mean . . . you relayed the conversation, but I'm just assuring I wouldn't be stepping on anyone's toes if . . . you know?" He still had his head down.

Noah was relieved that Leroy wasn't interested in Catherine, but his protectiveness for his sister kicked in as he considered his answer. "*Nee*, Ruth is not married or spoken for." In truth, he wasn't sure anyone could pin down his sister. She was a free spirit and opinionated but probably the kindest person he'd ever known. Even if she had scared away almost every man who had attempted to court her. But he'd noticed her reaction to Leroy. And she'd voiced it to Catherine.

Even though he was relieved that Leroy was interested in Ruth, and not Catherine, he couldn't bless any kind of potential courtship without knowing more about this man. And the more he thought about it, it seemed pointless considering they were all enroute to somewhere else. "Where are you headed?" he finally asked.

"Not far from here. Orleans. But too far for *mei* horse to make it in this weather." He shook his head. "All this snow and ice is unusual for this time of year."

Noah nodded, recalling what Catherine had said. "*Ya,*

Catherine said the same thing." He heard the way her name slid off his tongue.

Leroy grinned. "You fancy her, *ya*? And it sounds like she has taken to you as well even though there are challenges."

"I don't know her. I just got here." It was true, but if there was love at first sight, he'd witnessed it with Catherine. He couldn't stop thinking about overhearing the conversation between his sister and Catherine. At first, he'd meant to busy himself in the kitchen, but once he'd heard his name, his ear had stayed tuned. "If this weather doesn't clear, we might be stuck here for Thanksgiving Day."

Leroy smiled, nodded at the fireplace, then smiled at Noah. "A warm fire, two beautiful women, and a home-cooked meal . . . there could be worse places to be."

Noah had looked forward to seeing his family, even though he didn't know them very well, but he couldn't disagree and found himself hoping the weather didn't improve. He wasn't keen on a stranger showing such an immediate interest in his sister, but at least they were all under the same roof where he could keep an eye on Leroy and make sure he didn't have any indecent intentions. So far, Leroy seemed like a decent fellow.

Ruth entered the room a few moments later. "Hello," she said as she whizzed through with her head down, glancing only briefly at Leroy before she disappeared.

Wow, Noah thought to himself. That wasn't normal for his outspoken, confident sister. He was tempted to verbalize his thoughts to Leroy, but he'd said too much already. Both Noah and Leroy were attracted to two women. It wasn't anything more than that. Although the feelings seemed to be reciprocated, it was hard not to speculate about the possibilities—with challenges, as Leroy had said.

They both startled when Catherine walked into the room and asked if they needed anything, saying that she, her grandmother, and Ruth were preparing supper.

"*Nee*, we appreciate the hospitality, especially under the circumstances," Leroy said.

"Is there anything we can do to help around here?" Noah hoped she would respond in a way that would allow him to be close to her.

She raised an eyebrow and grinned. "As a matter of fact, there is." Then she winked at him, and he knew he was putty in her hands, for as long as God graced him with her presence.

CHAPTER 8

*N*oah held his breath and waited.

"There is extra firewood in the barn," Catherine said. "Perhaps you could bring some more logs into the *haus*. I hate to ask since it's still—"

"Of course," Leroy said before Noah did, turning Catherine's attention to him.

"*Ya*, happy to," Noah added as he stood alongside Leroy, smiling at Catherine when she finally turned his way.

They donned hats and coats, then slipped into their boots by the door. Out in the barn, Noah said, "I feel like I've been given a love potion." Then he looked at Leroy with huge regret that he'd voiced his feelings. "Uh, sorry. I don't know what made me say that."

"Don't apologize." Leroy picked up two logs, then paused. "And please don't take offense when I say that I feel the same way with regard to Ruth." He bowed his head slightly. "She's your *schweschder*, and I mean no disrespect."

Noah had two logs under his arms as he sat on a bale of hay, then balanced the logs in his lap. "Did you drink anything at The Peony Inn?"

Leroy bent at the waist before he straightened and laughed. "You're kidding, right?"

"Of course," Noah said, hearing the lack of conviction in his voice.

"Although . . ." Leroy lowered his two logs onto the ground, then also sat on a bale of hay, facing Noah with his hands on his knees. "There were six people in the main room at The Peony Inn. Two other couples, and an older gentleman that I think was an owner's husband." He looked directly at Noah. "But I'm the only one that Lizzie served hot tea." He paused. "It tasted funny, but I didn't want to say anything."

Noah thought for a few seconds. "Was it before or after your *interview?*"

"After." Leroy's eyebrows narrowed. "But there's no way . . . right?"

Noah laughed, but then stopped abruptly. "I don't believe in that kind of magic." He waved an arm dismissively. "Potions and such."

His people were known to be superstitious, and some of the elders believed in all kinds of strange rituals that didn't cross a biblical line but that were still odd. He could recall a friend of his grandmother who practiced powwowing, a combination of folk magic and traditional medicine, sometimes including herbal recipes. Noah knew there were mixed feelings about the few Amish folks still practicing powwowing. His grandmother—and the rest of his family—had never bought into the outdated tradition, often referred to as *braucherei*.

But as he thought back to his brief time at The Peony Inn, those vintage practices caused him to ponder. "Uh . . . the small woman, Lizzie, I believe . . . she brought me some tea, told Ruth she didn't have any more, and after apologizing, she brought Ruth a glass of lemonade."

Both men looked at each other, before they both burst out laughing. "Hogwash!" Leroy picked up his two logs, then moved toward the barn exit. "I don't believe in *braucherei*."

"I don't either," Noah said as he followed Leroy while toting his own logs.

But neither man said anything as they faced off with the cold and made their way to the house.

Back inside, after an awkward silence, and way too much thinking about nonsense like potions and powwowing, Noah stoked the fire right before Ruth emerged from the kitchen. "Supper is ready." She made the announcement without smiling, then tucked her chin and shuffled back toward the kitchen.

Noah watched her rush away. Since when did his sister become so introverted and seemingly shy? Where was her sharp tongue and witty banter? Maybe the lemonade had been spiked, too, since she couldn't even look at Leroy. Noah smiled to himself, shook his head, and slowly stood up. Leroy hadn't even shown up at The Peony Inn when he and Ruth left, so there wouldn't have been any point to lace Ruth's lemonade with something to make her lovesick. He forced the silly thoughts from his mind.

"What are you thinking?" Leroy whispered as he sidled up to Noah.

Noah shrugged. "*Mei schweschder* is acting weird as I explained." He grinned. "I was thinking maybe the older ladies at the inn spiked her lemonade, too, as silly as it sounds. But they hadn't even met you, so however far-fetched the idea, it wouldn't make sense that they would play matchmaker between you and Ruth."

Leroy grabbed Noah's arm and edged him to the right so that they weren't in view of the kitchen. "That's not exactly true. I had checked into the inn. I saw you and Ruth arrive while I was in the barn tending to *mei* horse. And when I went back inside, a taller woman—Esther, I think—told me they were all booked up, and she apologized for the mistake. Then sent me here."

Noah ran a hand through his hair, unable to keep a grin from surfacing. He locked eyes with Leroy. "You know, this is *ab im kopp*, these thoughts of powwowing and potions." Leroy nodded. "But I do know one thing. *Mei schweschder* can't look at you, and that only signifies one thing in *mei* mind."

Leroy frowned. "What's that?"

"She's taken a fancy to you, and she doesn't know how to cope with it." Noah grinned. "Ruth is normally very outspoken and witty. She's unsettled around you in a way I've never seen her behave."

Leroy sighed. "None of us know each other. But something sparked for me the moment I saw Ruth."

Noah leaned closer to Leroy and whispered. "We probably shouldn't say anything about this to the women, any mention of love potions or powwowing."

"Agreed." Leroy nodded before they both headed toward the kitchen.

CATHERINE FOLDED her hands in front of her, happy that her grandmother seemed okay. The table was filled with a lavish meal of meatloaf, mashed potatoes, glazed carrots, black-eyed peas, chow-chow, jams and jellies, and an apple pie that Catherine had in the freezer and had re-heated. She was saving her best China for Thanksgiving Day, but she'd chosen a lovely set of white dishes that set off her fall centerpiece atop a tan tablecloth. It was nice to lay out such a spread for more than just her and her grandmother.

"This looks wonderful," Noah said as he smiled at her.

Catherine felt herself blush. "*Danki*, it's nothing fancy."

Noah and Leroy sat next to each other. Catherine's grandmother sat at one end of the table, Catherine sat across from Noah, and Ruth sat across the table from Leroy.

They all bowed their heads in silent prayer, as was customary. Catherine looked up first, then Ruth, then the others.

The men filled their plates and dug in right away. Catherine's grandmother placed her usual small helping of each item on her plate, then took tiny bites. Ruth had served herself a little of everything, as had Catherine when the plates and bowls were passed around, but Ruth mostly moved her food around on her plate without eating.

After no one said anything for a while, Catherine said, "Perhaps we can all share in evening devotions after the meal?"

Everyone nodded except Ruth. The woman was so rigid and tense that Catherine worried Ruth might fall out of her chair if she didn't start to at least breathe. She gently nudged her, and Ruth came alive with a gasp.

"Sorry," she said before she lowered her head again.

Leroy smiled and couldn't keep his eyes off Ruth. Despite how uncomfortable Ruth clearly was, it was sweet the way they both seemed taken with each other. When Catherine shifted her gaze to Noah, he was watching her in between bites. She regretted winking at him earlier. When had she become so flirtatious?

AFTER THE MEAL, Noah repeatedly thanked Catherine. It was overkill, he knew. He even offered to help clean the kitchen, which she politely declined, saying that she and her grandmother would take care of it. Ruth hadn't even argued, only began a trek upstairs to her room.

Leroy didn't hide his disappointment as he watched Ruth ascending the stairs, his blue eyes reflecting a sheen of regret as the lines on his forehead creased. Noah hoped Ruth would rejoin them for devotions later. He recalled his time with Catherine fondly while also fighting off the silly notion that Lizzie had slipped something into his and Leroy's tea, possibly even into Ruth's lemonade. Preposterous as it was, he needed to talk to his sister..

"I'm going to check on Ruth," he told Leroy as his new

friend sat in one of the rocking chairs and picked up the gardening magazine, again appearing to flip the pages too fast to be reading anything. He'd shared at lunch that he was a farmer by trade and owned four hundred acres where he lived in Orleans. Right now, his mind appeared somewhere else.

Noah knocked on the closed door to Ruth's room. "*Wie bischt.* It's me. Are you okay?" He eased the door open and found her sitting on the bed, a glum expression on her face.

She sat taller and lifted her chin, resembling the Ruth he knew. "I'm perfectly fine."

Noah smirked. "Really? Because if I didn't know better, I'd think there is such a spark between you and Leroy that if you held hands, you'd probably electrocute each other."

He opted not to tell her that he'd eavesdropped.

Ruth's eyebrows lifted as she pressed her lips together. "You don't know what you're talking about."

Noah sighed. "Ruth, why can't you admit that you're attracted to that man?"

"I don't even know that man!" She groaned, then put her head in her hands. "I can't be around anyone who makes me feel this scattered," she said in a muffled voice before she looked up at him with wide eyes. "This has never happened to me before, and I-I . . . I just can't face him."

"Ruth, you should find out if there is something there." Noah sat beside her on the bed.

"As we've discussed, we live a very long way from these people." She paused and held up one finger. "If I was even inclined to pursue anything."

His sister stood and walked to the window. "It's stopped snowing."

Noah had noticed that after supper. "*Ya*, I know." He swallowed hard about the possibility of them having to leave.

"We should probably think about leaving early tomorrow morning so we can make Thanksgiving dinner with Fannie and Amos."

"We wouldn't make it until late afternoon." He paused, rubbed his chin. "Besides, we don't really know Fannie and Amos any more than we know the people downstairs. And we've never met their *kinner*."

"Which is exactly why we should make every effort to get there." Ruth sighed.

"We can't control the weather. *Gott* must want us here for some reason. Maybe it's so that Catherine and her grandmother aren't alone on Thanksgiving."

Ruth huffed. "You just want to be around Catherine."

Noah shrugged. "And I admit that. Why can't you admit that you'd like to get to know Leroy?"

"I told you." She looked away from him. "He makes me feel very unsettled, like I have butterflies in *mei* stomach."

Again, Noah recalled the conversation he'd overheard. But instead of telling Ruth, maybe things needed to evolve organically, even though Noah and Leroy had a head's up as to how everyone was feeling.

Noah grinned. "Um . . . back at The Peony Inn, did your lemonade taste . . . odd?"

"Why would you ask me that?" His sister raised her chin even more defiantly than before.

"Just wondering." Noah sighed before he moved toward the door. "I guess we will see how the weather is and decide what we want to do in the morning."

He was almost out the door when Ruth said, "Noah?"

"*Ya*?" He turned to face her and waited an unusually long time before she spoke.

"*Mei* lemonade did taste strange."

Noah swallowed hard. "Leroy said his tea didn't taste right, and neither did mine. Maybe we are all suffering . . ." He grinned. ". . . or enjoying . . . some sort of potion one of the women at The Peony Inn slipped into our drinks. Like a love potion. Apparently, the sisters are well-known as matchmakers around here."

He cringed on the inside as he waited for Ruth to question how he could know that, realizing he had practically confessed to listening in on her conversation with Catherine, but she seemed deep in thought, twitching her mouth back and forth.

Noah sat silently as he waited for her to speak words of wisdom, to debunk such silliness, but then she burst out laughing before stilling her expression. "Maybe so," she said in a serious voice as her eyebrows narrowed.

CHAPTER 9

*C*atherine read from the Bible. She knew
Philippians 4:6 by heart—*Do not be anxious about
anything, but in everything, by prayer and petition, with
thanksgiving, present your requests to God.* It was relevant
and always spoke to Catherine's heart, but more so today,
it seemed.

It was easy to sneak peeks at everyone while she read.
She was sitting on the couch in between Ruth and Noah,
and her grandmother and Leroy were in the two rocking
chairs on the other side of the coffee table. It was as if
everyone, but her grandmother, were playing hide n' seek
with their eyes, herself included. She'd look at Noah and
find him staring at her before she looked away, then Ruth
would lock eyes with Leroy, only to shift her eyes when
he looked back at her.

Her grandmother had been quietly knitting while
Catherine read aloud, but when she stowed her knitting
needles in the basket beside her and stood, Catherine
stopped reading.

"Jessica, you are putting me to sleep." She put her hands on her hips. "That is not the way the scriptures are to be read. We've had this conversation before." She pressed her wrinkled hands to her chest. "Invoke enthusiasm, and the Holy Spirit will fill your heart. You're not reading the newspaper. Treat the readings from the Bible as they are meant to be read." Then she pointed a finger at Noah, then Leroy. "And another thing. There was a time in *mei* life when single men would not be allowed to stay under the same roof as single women. I expect both of you men to be respectful of these women." She scrunched up her face. "No canoodling."

Catherine's face burned from the heat of pure embarrassment, but she pressed her lips firmly together, unsure what to say. None of them were teenagers.

"Ma'am, you have nothing to worry about," Noah said after he'd glanced Catherine's way.

Ruth's chin almost touched her chest when she lowered her head. The beginning of a smile tipped the corners of Leroy's mouth. After a momentary contemplation, Catherine acknowledged to herself that it wasn't that bizarre of a comment. She didn't know these people even though she felt like she'd known them all her life; possibly she had been awaiting their arrival in some obscure way. Their presence was a gift for however long the Lord graced her with their company.

After her grandmother excused herself, Catherine cleared her throat. "Shall I go on?"

Leroy looped his thumbs beneath his suspenders from where he was sitting in the rocking chair. "In *mei* family, we read from the Bible, but we also have discussions about what certain scriptures mean to us." He glanced around the room. "It's just an idea, maybe a way to learn more about each other." He shrugged, then repeated, "It's just an idea."

Catherine loved this concept. What better way for them to get to know each other? She searched her mind for an appropriate verse. "What about Ephesians 4:29? Do not let any unwholesome talk come out of your mouths, but only what is helpful for building others up according to their needs, that it may benefit those who listen."

She glanced around the room, first at Noah, to her left on the couch. He smiled and nodded, and Leroy also gave an approving nod from the rocking chair. She turned her head right, to where Ruth was beside her on the couch. "I'll go first," Ruth said, slightly smiling.

Catherine's eyes widened in surprise more than she would have liked. Ruth had been so rigid and quiet. "Okay," Catherine said softly.

Ruth reached for Catherine's hand and squeezed. "I think this scripture is about family life. The way I see it, you are a very *gut* granddaughter, and it is evident in your eyes how much you *lieb* your *mammi*. Despite your challenges, *Gott* will lead you onto the path He has planned for you. That's what I think about these lines that you read."

Catherine blinked back tears. It was such a sweet, endearing thing to say. And something that she struggled to believe. "*Danki*," she said softly, giving Ruth's hand a squeeze and happy the woman seemed to be coming back to life.

Ruth had attempted to build up Catherine, and it felt

like it was her turn to respond in kind to one of the people in the room whom she barely knew. She reminded herself that this was why she chose this scripture. As she turned to Noah, his deep brown eyes locked with hers.

"*Danki* for helping me with *Mammi*. You are gentle, kind, and I appreciate it." She felt her cheeks blush at the same time Noah's did.

He nodded. "I am happy to help." He cleared his throat before he looked at his sister. "Ruth, that was beautiful what you said to Catherine, and I agree." Pausing, he grinned. "And it's nice to see you returning to normal," he muffled the words, but they all heard him.

Ruth stiffened from her spot on the couch, folded her hands in her lap, and leaned around Catherine to scowl at her brother. "I have no idea what you're talking about." She shot him a dagger with her eyes before she leaned back.

"I guess I'll go next." Leroy took a deep breath. "I want to thank Catherine for taking us into her home, strangers, who come together to worship and uplift. We accept *Gott's* plan for us, and this evening we bless each other with the gift of new friendships."

Catherine bowed her head and silently thanked God again for bringing these people into her life, if only for a while. Ruth had fallen silent again. They all had. They'd basically thanked each other for kindnesses that had occurred. But Catherine—and now Ruth—were aware of Lizzie and Esther's matchmaking schemes. The sisters did have a way of knowing folks who would make a good match. She'd barely had the thought when Noah's hand brushed against hers before he looped his pinky finger with hers, out of sight, but a definite sign of shared feelings. She recalled winking at him and cringed on the inside. She was torn between enjoying these precious moments or cutting it off cold before it could even start. Since it—*they*—had nowhere to go.

"Leroy . . ." Ruth spoke softly with a tremble in her voice. "How can we pray and uplift you today?"

Catherine smiled on the inside again. Ruth wasn't the vivacious woman who had shown up on her doorstep, but she seemed to be working her way back despite the butterflies in her stomach that she had mentioned.

Leroy gazed into Ruth's eyes for a long time, as if Catherine and Noah weren't even in the room. "Your presence uplifts me."

Catherine bit her bottom lip to stifle any outburst. This man was incredibly bold, but he sounded so sincere. Ruth's jaw hung open, presumably as affected as Catherine thought.

Leroy smiled. "I think you are the most beautiful woman I've ever seen, and—"

Ruth jumped to her feet. "Stop!" She locked eyes with her brother, then Catherine, and lastly Leroy. "Something is going on."

"Uh, Ruth." Noah let go of Catherine's finger and stood, seemingly concerned about his sister's outburst.

"Those women . . ." Ruth shook her head until strands of dark hair spilled from beneath her prayer covering. "What were their names?" She knocked her knuckles against each other while rapping her foot against the wood floor. She snapped a finger. "Lizzie and Esther!"

Catherine froze. Where was Ruth going with this? Was

she about to share the stories she'd told her about Lizzie and Esther?

"Remember, I said *mei* lemonade tasted funny?" She directed the question to her brother. Catherine didn't remember Ruth saying anything to her. "And you said your tea tasted odd, the tea you had at The Peony Inn. Right, Noah?"

Catherine stood when Leroy did. "*Mei* tea wasn't *gut* either. Tasted funny," Leroy said, but with a smirk on his face, almost as if he was just playing along.

Ruth put her hands on her hips and turned to Catherine. "Those two sweet older women drugged us!"

"What?" Catherine wanted to close the huge can of worms she'd opened.

Ruth pointed a finger at her. "Noah really likes you. I really like Leroy. And he seems smitten with me. You sure look at Noah with tenderness. How could such feelings develop so quickly?"

Catherine was speechless. She was the one who had told Ruth the story about the love potion and how Lizzie and Esther were notorious matchmakers. She couldn't believe Ruth had snapped this way and was telling the tale. She was tempted to jump into the mix and tell the group that she was drawn to Noah, but she hadn't drunk the tea or lemonade, so she stayed quiet.

"You really like me?" Leroy said with a wide grin that showed his perfectly white teeth. He was handsome, but not in the same rugged way as Noah.

Ruth marched over to him and slammed her hands to her hips. "Of course I like you. I drank the magic potion." She blew wild strands of hair from her face.

"Wait, wait, wait." Catherine raised both her hands, palms out defensively. "Ruth, I shouldn't have ever mentioned that Lizzie and Esther love to play matchmaker. And there is a problem with your analogy." She crossed her arms across her chest, deciding she would enjoy the moment after all. It might be short-lived, but it was hers. "I didn't drink the tea." She grinned as she cut her eyes in Ruth's direction. "Or the lemonade."

Noah edged closer to her. "What are you saying?" He and Leroy exchanged an all-knowing look, even grinning, which made Catherine wonder if either of the men had overheard her conversation with Ruth.

Catherine turned to face him but stayed quiet. Either way, surely it was obvious without her stating it aloud. But she said it again. "I didn't drink the tea or any lemonade."

"She's right!" Ruth's eyes were wild, but Leroy couldn't stop looking at her and smiling. "You like Noah on his own merit." She gave a taut nod of her head, then grinned.

The old Ruth was back in full force, and somehow this devotion time had turned into a conversation that was surely unfit for them to be having at all, especially now.

Catherine glanced around their foursome, everyone standing. Then she began to laugh. She couldn't remember the last time she'd been this tickled by anything so peculiar.

Leroy shrugged and started to laugh also. Then he picked up a lit lantern on the fireplace mantel since dusk was settling around them. "Ruth, I think we should go discuss our newfound *lieb* for each other. Would you like to join me in the kitchen, perhaps for some *kaffi*?"

Catherine put a hand to her forehead. *What is happening?*

Ruth shrugged. "We might as well . . . before this magic potion wears off."

As Ruth strutted toward the kitchen, Leroy held the lantern high and followed in her shadow.

Catherine realized she still had her hand on her forehead, so she lowered it, standing and facing Noah, the most gorgeous man she'd ever met. And that she could never have. Her grandmother might not have her mental faculties, but she was otherwise healthy and could live another ten or twenty years. It was Catherine's responsibility to take care of her. She pushed back at her anger toward her parents, which was building with every breath she took in Noah's presence. She opened her mouth to say something, but not only was the situation silly, she feared that anything she said would sound equally as fatuous.

"I don't believe in magic potions." Noah inched closer to her. "I believe in *Gott's* intentions, and however bizarre it may seem, we are all here, under your roof for a reason. Maybe several reasons."

Catherine couldn't decipher whether he was saying that he wasn't interested in her by brushing off the notion that Lizzie might have spiked their drinks or if he was trying to tell her that he really did have feelings for her.

"Let's sit." Noah pointed to the couch. "The look on your face makes me wonder if you might faint."

Catherine couldn't argue as she went to the sofa and sat. Noah sat right beside her, reached for her hand, and held it tightly. "What are you concerned about at this very moment?"

She closed her eyes and savored this memory, how good her hand felt in his, how handsome and kind he was. But she owed him the truth.

"I don't believe in magic potions either. We are mature adults, not adolescents." She paused, sighing. "*Mei* concern at this very moment is that if I allow myself to fall for you, it has nowhere to go. You live far away, and I am committed to taking care of *mei grandmammi* for as long as she needs me to."

Noah nodded and was quiet.

Catherine wanted to snatch her hand away and run to the safety of her bedroom where temptations of falling in love didn't linger nearby. It felt cruel for God to drop the perfect man at her doorstep, only to have him leave.

Noah let go of her hand, then cupped her cheeks and gazed into her eyes. Would he offer some words of wisdom or just kiss her because the opportunity had presented itself? She couldn't remember when she'd last kissed a man.

$\mathcal{N}$oah's heart ignored Catherine's words as his lips met with hers, refusing to corral whatever he was feeling. And as she returned the kiss with passion that only comes from inside, from the heart, he knew he was in trouble. Because she was right. He lived in Pennsylvania. She lived here in Indiana and tended to her grandmother. Would they share a brief romance, then walk away from each other forever? Why would God allow that to happen?

After making out like teenagers, oblivious to what might be going on in the kitchen, Noah eased away from her, then brushed back strands of her hair, the color of chestnuts, which reminded him of the holidays. "I like you, Catherine," he said. "And I do hear what you're saying. I've had those thoughts since I first met you."

Noah couldn't leave his family. He was sure of it. Not only was his family close to each other, but he worked with his father at the construction company they owned.

He was the only son to help and carry on the business someday.

Catherine couldn't leave her grandmother.

She lowered her eyes, her long dark lashes brushing against high cheekbones. He wanted to tell her something that made sense, but this didn't compute. "Maybe we shouldn't think on it too much. We are both old enough to know what is at stake." *Our hearts*, he thought to himself. "Tomorrow is Thanksgiving, and I'm thankful to have met you, no matter what."

She offered up a weak smile. "I'm thankful that you, Ruth, and Leroy showed up at our home. It's been so nice to have this time with all of you."

Catherine was shying away from the predicament they were in and finding good in the situation. That's what Noah needed to do also.

"Maybe it will be the best Thanksgiving ever." He smiled, thinking about sharing the holiday with her even if it meant foregoing time with his relatives, or postponing it

"The weather," she said softly as she lowered her chin and chewed her bottom lip for a few moments. "It's not snowing, and I think the weather is supposed to continue to improve. I-I guess you'll be leaving in the morning?"

Noah held her hand in his. "I suppose we should be looking forward to seeing our relatives, but . . ." He paused, sighing. "We don't really know them, and *Gott* seems to have other plans for our visit here.. If Ruth is on board, I'm thinking we might stay here for the holiday, if that's all right."

Her expression brightened right away, but suddenly, Noah's chest tightened. "Excuse me, but I really need to go around the corner and check on Ruth. Some people say I'm so protective of her because we are twins, but . . ." He sighed. "I don't know Leroy. He seems like a nice man, but . . ."

"I understand." Catherine nodded before Noah stood to go check on his sister.

He walked with heavy steps as a warning before he entered the room, but it turned out he had nothing to fear. Ruth was sitting across the table from Leroy, each with a cup of coffee, the light of the lantern between them dancing in shadows above the kitchen table.

"*Wie bischt, bruder*. Did you come to check on me?" Ruth flashed him an all-knowing smile. She'd either succumbed to the improbable idea that her drink had been laced with love potion, and she was going along with it, or she genuinely liked Leroy but had accepted the fact that they probably wouldn't see each other again. Either way, she seemed back to her old self.

"Uh, *nee*." He swallowed hard as he struggled for any other reason to come into the kitchen. "*Ach, ya*, I guess I did come to check on you." He shrugged before looking at Leroy. "Sorry," he said.

"*Nee*, it's honorable. I respect that." He turned to Ruth. "And I respect your *schweschder*. She's been telling me about your family in Pennsylvania."

Noah took a deep breath and blew it out slowly. "Okay, I'm just going to . . ." He pointed over his shoulder. ". . . get back to Catherine." He felt like he was at an Amish singing, usually reserved for teenagers, but a much larger gathering. As youngsters, couples often tried to sneak off together.

His sister smiled. "Don't worry so much, Noah. *Gott* has us. All the time."

When he returned, Catherine was standing and staring out the window into the yard, lit only by the moonlight, the shadows of the trees swaying in a light breeze. The weather already seemed better this evening, even in the darkness.

"Everything okay?" she asked over her shoulder.

"*Ya*, they just seem to be enjoying each other's company and getting to know each other." He grinned. "Sound familiar?"

She smiled back at him as they both sat on the couch again, with the crackling of the fire, the warmth of his hand in hers, and a great sense of peace filling a space in Noah's heart that he hadn't known was empty.

After a few moments, Noah asked, "Do you have any idea why your *mammi* calls you Jessica sometimes?"

"*Nee*, I don't." She sighed. "It started two years ago on and off. We don't know anyone by that name."

"When she mentioned the canoodling, it was almost like she was talking to a child." Noah scratched his chin.

"That's what I've thought almost every time she has called me Jessica." Catherine turned to him and locked eyes. "I've thought of every scenario." She shook her head. "I told you about *mei* parents leaving our district." She glanced his way, and he nodded. "I've often wondered if they had another child, maybe a girl born before they were married. Even if that were the case, there would have been heartache to bear, but I don't know any of our people who would give a *boppli* up for adoption. I've known people to adopt from the *Englisch*, but not the other way around."

"Maybe it was someone she was *gut* friends with as a child," Noah said. "Or maybe it was even a character in a book."

Catherine shrugged. "I don't know. I've thought about those things too." She blinked back tears, which tugged at Noah's heart, but he still had one thing left to say.

"Ruth was right. We've seen our parents' friends go through this type of thing, and it does get worse, I'm afraid." He gently touched her arm. "Catherine, it's noble that you're practically giving up your life for your *mammi*, but I think you are going to need help at some point."

"Maybe." She leaned over and unexpectedly kissed him softly on the mouth. "Right now, I don't want to think about it," she whispered before she kissed him again.

As Noah leaned into her, he worried again how he would walk away from this woman.

"Jessica, what in the world?"

Catherine gasped as she fled Noah's embrace. "*Mammi*, what are you doing up?" She jumped to her feet.

Noah also leaped to his feet as embarrassment rushed through his veins, then landed in his chest with a hard thud. "I meant no disrespect," he said to Catherine's grandmother with both palms facing her, feeling like a teenager instead of the twenty-seven-year-old man that he was.

Catherine's grandmother pointed a finger at Noah. I'm keeping *mei* eye on you." The older woman squinted her eyes at him before she turned to Catherine. "Catherine, we will discuss this later, but we must start the turkey. It is best to slow cook it all night long. I set the alarm on *mei* clock so I would get up and get it in the oven."

As the small woman marched toward the kitchen, Noah ran ahead and blocked her path. "Wait, Mary Marie, I want to apologize again." He spoke loudly to make sure Leroy and Ruth heard him, in case their innocent chat had turned into something more.

Before Catherine's grandmother could say anything, Leroy and Ruth emerged from the kitchen, both looking flustered, and Ruth's prayer covering was on sideways. Noah was tempted to laugh at the entire situation, but when he looked over his shoulder at Catherine, he realized nothing was funny about this scenario. Her cheeks were flushed as she blinked back tears, slowly walking to her grandmother until she was right in front of her. Leroy and Ruth stood side by side and didn't say a word. Noah chose to watch silently as well.

"*Mammi*, I will help you get the turkey in the oven. No one is doing anything wrong here."

Noah looked down at the floor. Maybe they had all gotten a little carried away. Perhaps Ruth and Leroy were doing the same thing as he and Catherine, getting in as much time with each other as they could before they had to say goodbye.

"*Mammi*," Catherine went on. "These people are guests in our home. Remember? Lizzie from The Peony Inn didn't have enough room for them, so they each have a room upstairs."

Her grandmother frowned as her eyebrows narrowed

on her forehead, deepening the lines of time. "I know that. I'm not crazy."

Noah saw the relief in Catherine's face as she exhaled whatever breath she must have been holding. "I don't think you're crazy, *Mammi*."

Her grandmother grunted. "Humph. I should hope not."

"I'd be happy to help you with the turkey and anything else for tomorrow's meal," Ruth said sheepishly as she cast her eyes toward Noah, a clear indication that they would not be traveling to see their relatives tomorrow, even if the weather allowed it. "We would like to enjoy the holiday with you if that's all right. We wouldn't be able to get to our relative's *haus* until late afternoon or early evening, so I'm sure they will understand if we are delayed a day or two." She glanced at Leroy.

"I would enjoy celebrating the holiday with you all as well," Leroy said before smiling at Ruth.

"As Jessica said, you are guests in our home, and we would *lieb* for you all to celebrate Thanksgiving with us."

Catherine clenched her fists at her sides before she gently latched on to her grandmother's small arms. "*Mammi*, I am not Jessica! Look at me. I am your granddaughter, Catherine!"

Noah didn't move or even breathe. The silence was thick, only the ticking of the clock on the mantel in the next room. He wanted to run to Catherine when she lowered her head and dropped her hands to her sides. "I'm sorry," she said. "I'm Catherine."

Noah wasn't sure if she was apologizing to her guests or to her grandmother, but his heart ached for her. What torture it must be to have a loved one not know who she was all the time, to fade away from life at the hands of such a savage disease.

Everyone was silent when Mary Marie cupped Catherine's chin and lifted her eyes to hers. Catherine and her grandmother's cheeks were moist from tears. It was heartbreaking every time Mary Marie opened her mouth to speak but didn't say anything. Noah thought everyone in the room was holding their breath the same way that he was.

Finally, Mary Marie spoke. "*Mei* sweet *maedel*, I know you are . . ." She paused, and Noah said a silent prayer that she would remember her granddaughter's name. ". . . you are Catherine. You are *mei* beautiful granddaughter. Sometimes, I get confused or forgetful, but I know you are Catherine. Please never forget that, even as I continue to get worse."

Catherine pulled her grandmother into her arms. "I *lieb* you, *Mamma*."

"And I *lieb* you, Catherine."

After a long embrace, they separated, and Noah was thankful that the night ended on a good note for Catherine and Mary Marie.

"*Danki* for having us," Ruth said. "Can I help you with anything, preparation of the meal?"

"*Nee*." Catherine's grandmother pressed her palms together as if in prayer, then smiled, her eyes twinkling in the softly lit room. "Tomorrow will be a blessed day, and our *haus* will be filled with those who *Gott* has sent here to share Thanksgiving."

"*Danki*," Leroy said. "It will be a wonderful day."

Clearly, he wasn't focusing on the weather either. Maybe he didn't have plans for Thanksgiving. He had mentioned getting home to Orleans but nothing about spending the holiday with family.

Mary Marie glanced at each one of them, clearly pondering what she might have on her mind. "And it will mean the world to me when you all meet Jessica," she said, mostly to Catherine, who dropped her gaze to the floor again.

"*Mammi*, I'm Catherine," she said barely above a whisper.

Her grandmother smiled. "I know that *mei maedel*. We just had a conversation about that. Jessica won't be here until tomorrow." She began to exit the room but looked over her shoulder. "So, let's not forget to set a place for her."

Then she left the room. And Noah pulled Catherine into a hug.

CHAPTER 11

*C*atherine eyed the chocolate mocha brownie dessert she'd just iced. Her grandmother said it was her signature dessert, and Catherine wanted this Thanksgiving Day to be special in every way.

She eyed the offerings she, her grandmother, and Ruth had already laid out. Cornbread stuffing, mashed potatoes, sweet potatoes, peas, Indiana's finest sweet corn, rolls, chow-chow, and jams and jellies.

"Everything will be perfect," her grandmother said as she stood back and inspected the spread of food.

"*Ya*, it will," Ruth said as she clasped her hands in front of her. "It will be a special day."

All three women had been up since five o'clock that morning preparing the food.

Catherine took the large bird from the oven and placed the turkey in the middle of the table, then she also took a few moments to eye the other desserts.

Pies, cookies, and cakes were on the counter. Her

grandmother's pumpkin cheesecake looked beautiful, and Catherine hoped her grandmother had been able to follow the recipe correctly. She recalled the last time she'd prepared what Catherine thought was her best dessert, the time she only added one package of cream cheese instead of three packages the recipe called for. If that was the case, Catherine knew her guests would be forgiving. And Catherine was pretty sure she'd prepared the pecan pie her grandmother requested to near perfection by following the recipe. Ruth had helped with several side dishes but also prepared a key lime pie that she said was her specialty. Catherine was thrilled to have all the ingredients on hand, especially the limes.

Noah and Leroy came into the kitchen and complimented the enormous offering of food. Catherine's heart swelled, so pleased to be having guests for this special day.

"Ruth, did you call Fannie and Amos to let them know we won't be coming today?" Noah glanced at Catherine, and while she felt badly about Noah and Ruth not attending their family gathering for the holiday, it wasn't enough to squash the joy she felt at having them here.

"*Ya*, I did. They had suspected we might be delayed due to the weather." Ruth glanced at Leroy with a twinkle in her eyes. Leroy hadn't mentioned any family plans, but he was clearly content being here based on the way he looked at Ruth.

"I think we are ready," Catherine's grandmother announced. After everyone was seated and silent prayer was observed, Catherine cleared her throat. "And I would like to add how happy *Mammi* and I are to have all of you joining us." She glanced at Noah, then Ruth and Leroy, who all resembled the unconventional family she hadn't known she needed until now. She thought briefly about her parents, wondering what each of them were doing for the holiday. But the thought faded as quickly as it had developed. For today, her family felt complete, and she wasn't going to let the past smother her joy.

"I'd like to offer up an additional prayer for safe travels for Jessica." Her grandmother cast her eyes downward as her eyes clouded with uneasiness. "I don't understand why she isn't here yet."

All eyes avoided the empty chair and place setting Catherine's grandmother had reminded her to set out.

Anguish for her grandmother seared Catherine's heart, and she wished she could snap her fingers and make this longing for her grandmother become a reality. *Better to change the subject.*

"Noah, would you do the honors of slicing the turkey?" Catherine stood from her chair across from this handsome man who would be leaving either later today or tomorrow.

"*Ya*, I'd *lieb* to." Noah stood, then walked to the opening where an empty chair and place setting awaited a person he feared would never show up, except in Mary Marie's mind.

"It's been a while," Noah said as he sliced into the turkey. "In truth, I can only recall carving a turkey on one occasion, when *mei* father had broken his wrist and asked me to stand in for him."

"I remember that Thanksgiving," Ruth said, grinning. "You completely botched the job."

Noah frowned at his sister. "I wouldn't call it botched."

"I'm sure it will be fine," Catherine said from her seat to his right as he did begin to bungle the job, slicing in the wrong direction, then carving into the middle of one of the turkey legs.

Catherine bit her bottom lip. She'd been known to do a much better job than Noah, but she wasn't about to say anything. "It all goes down the same," she finally said as the poor bird resembled a form of roadkill that smelled delicious.

Catherine glanced at her grandmother who didn't seem to notice Noah's dissection of the large bird. Instead, her grandmother leaned to her left so she could see out the window. She'd been staring in that direction ever since they'd sat down.

Ruth chuckled. "Noah, that poor bird is mess." She pointed at the turkey. "You're supposed to remove the breast to keep the skin intact, and you're not slicing in the right direction."

Noah's sister went on to criticize his efforts, but he took it in stride laughing along with her. Catherine was waiting for her grandmother to come unglued. The older woman could carve a turkey to perfection, but she had said earlier that the arthritis in her hands was acting up. She'd asked Catherine to ask one of the men to take on the job. Catherine wondered if she should have asked Leroy. But as Noah and Ruth continued to laugh, it was hard not to find the humor in the situation. Their table, topped with a white cloth, their best China, crystal glasses on full display, and white candles flickering atop silver candelabras was picture-perfect, except for the mutilation of the turkey.

Leroy jokingly asked, "Need any help, Noah?"

Noah stopped his actions, stared at the bird with an exaggerated frown, then chuckled. "Perhaps I wasn't the best choice for this job." He turned to Catherine, who had her hand over her mouth in an effort not to laugh. "Sorry, Catherine."

"*Nee*, it's fine," she said after she lowered her hand and grinned. Even if the turkey wasn't picture-perfect, Catherine was thrilled to be spending Thanksgiving Day with Noah, Ruth, and Leroy. She could tell Leroy and Ruth were smitten with each other by the way they looked at one another, smiling with the all-knowing calm of blossoming feelings. But surely, they were aware of the facts, the same as she and Noah. *Geography*.

No one said a word about the shafts of sunlight streaming through the window with no indication of looming rain, and the icy slush was almost completely melted.

As Noah continued to rip at the bird, and the side dishes lost the steam that had been rising, Catherine's grandmother seemed oblivious about the turkey. She continued to stare out the window. Catherine wondered what kind of disappointment her grandmother had coming. Maybe she wouldn't be upset at all, just carry on the way she often did when things became confusing.

"Noah." Ruth sighed. "Please give that turkey some dignity and just stop."

Catherine smiled at him, and his eyes twinkled when he looked back at her. "Catherine, again, I'm sorry about this." He waved a hand around the table. "Everything looks so nice, and I'm making a mess of this turkey."

"No worries at all. *Mammi* cooks the best turkeys. *Mei* only job is to put it in the oven and take it out. She does all the seasoning and stuffing. It will taste wonderful, no matter how it looks." She glanced at her grandmother, still expecting some sort of reaction about the turkey, but she continued to look around Noah and out the window. Catherine hoped she wouldn't stay so disappointed during this holiday meal. Perhaps she would just put it behind her and forget about it, like she did with so many other things. *A cruel condition, indeed.*

By the time Noah returned to his chair, they were all giggling, and even with a hacked-up turkey, this was the best Thanksgiving Catherine could remember having in a long time.

"Jessica should be here by now." Her grandmother looked over her shoulder at the clock on the wall. "She said she'd be here by noon, so I think we should wait a little longer."

It was already twelve-thirty. "*Mammi*, I don't think we should keep our guests waiting." Catherine's stomach growled as she spoke. "Perhaps there is a reason that . . ." She paused, swallowing back a lump in her throat. ". . . that Jessica isn't here yet. I'm sure she won't mind if we begin without her." Sometimes, it was best to go along with her.

"*Ya*, of course." Her grandmother seemed to force a smile. "Please, everyone, eat."

Their small group didn't waste any time passing bowls and retrieving chunks of turkey. Noah, Ruth, and Leroy raved about the food, and even though pride was a sin,

Catherine was bursting with delight until she noticed that her grandmother hadn't touched anything on her plate.

"*Mammi*, you have to eat." Catherine could see the hurt in the older woman's eyes, and it broke her heart. "I'm sure Jessica will be here soon." It was a lie, of course, but one she hoped God would forgive.

Her grandmother nodded as she took a small bite of mashed potatoes, then offered up a small smile in Catherine's direction.

When everyone exclaimed that they were full, Catherine reminded them about dessert. It would prolong their time at the table a little longer. Catherine was sure there wasn't anyone named Jessica who was going to magically appear, but a part of her held out hope that she was wrong. Her guests seemed to understand her plan, and they each opted for samples of all the desserts.

Catherine ate as slowly as she could. Her mocha brownie seemed to be a hit, she noticed, as everyone finished that dessert first, her grandmother included, but not without looking out the window in between bites. Ruth's key lime pie was wonderful, and Catherine noticed that Leroy had more than one helping.

Eventually, they couldn't stall any more. "*Mammi*, I'm sure Jessica is just running late. I'll clean all of this, and when she gets here, we can warm up a plate for her." Catherine held her breath. Her grandmother could shift into another realm faster than Catherine could keep up sometimes. She might forget all about Jessica and begin calling her granddaughter by that name again.

"I'd like to help Catherine clean up, Mary Marie." Ruth

placed a hand on Catherine's grandmother's hand. "Everything was wonderful."

"*Danki*, Ruth. Your key lime pie was delicious, and Catherine and I appreciate your help with the meal." Catherine's grandmother strained her neck to see out the window again before she looked back at Ruth. "If you're sure you don't mind, I think I'd like to take a short nap. I probably got up too early, and I'm a bit spent."

"Of course," Ruth said, smiling.

Catherine could hear the defeat in her grandmother's voice, and it saddened her, but overall, the meal had been wonderful, and without incident. For that, Catherine was thankful.

"We can help too," Noah said as he winked at Catherine, sending a welcomed warmth that ran the length of her body.

After Leroy echoed the same offer, Catherine agreed to all of them working together.

"Catherine?"

"*Ya, Mammi?*" Catherine stopped on her way to the refrigerator as she carried the chow-chow and a bottle of jam.

"You will wake me when Jessica arrives, *ya?*" Her bottom lip trembled as she blinked back tears. "I just don't understand."

"*Ya, Mammi.* I will wake you if . . . *when* . . . Jessica gets here." Catherine swallowed back the lump in her throat. She wasn't sure the woman had ever looked as sad as she did right now, except when Catherine's parents announced they were leaving the district and getting an English divorce.

Her grandmother shuffled out of the kitchen just as someone knocked loudly on the front door. Catherine looked at Ruth, then Noah, then Leroy. "*Nee*, it can't be," she said as she set down the jars in her hands, then left the room and followed her grandmother to the front door.

Catherine held her breath as her grandmother opened the door.

CHAPTER 12

*N*oah, Ruth, and Leroy peeked around the corner from the kitchen, waiting anxiously to see who had arrived.

"Could there really be a person named Jessica?" Ruth asked the men, who were both leaning over each of her shoulders. "Catherine doesn't seem to believe there is."

Noah stretched his neck until he could see over his sister's head. They were twins, but he had been taller than her since they were toddlers. "Whoever it is, Catherine is pushing the screen open so they can come in." He was pretty sure Leroy, and his sister, were holding their breath like he was.

"Wait a minute," Leroy said in a whisper. "Those are the two ladies who dumped *lieb* potion in our drinks."

Ruth gently elbowed him. "We don't know that for sure."

Noah didn't believe in such things. At least, he didn't think so. But the sisters were either the perfect match-makers or something else was in play.

The smaller of the two women began to speak softly. "Did it work? Are Noah and Catherine getting along? And what about Leroy and Ruth? Are they all still here?"

"That's Lizzie," Ruth said softly. "The other larger woman is Esther."

Noah and Leroy nodded as they tried to keep out of sight but also hear the conversation.

"Our guests at the inn just finished dessert, and since the weather cleared, we thought we would come to visit." Esther spoke louder than her sister.

Catherine put a finger to her lips as she ushered the women inside. "I'm not going to say that you didn't do well with your matchmaking efforts. But you took a big chance sending three people here that you barely knew." She shrugged. "Not to mention, I didn't know them."

Lizzie pointed upward. "*Gott* told me to. And they aren't serial killers or anything."

Noah had to put a hand over his mouth to keep from laughing. Leroy grunted a small laugh, but then moved to the side and stacked some dishes on the table, an effort to make it sound like they were cleaning the kitchen.

Ruth and Noah stayed in position, and Leroy rejoined them in a few seconds. "Did I miss anything?"

"*Nee*, not really. Just what you heard, that *Gott* told her to send the three of us here." Ruth smiled at Leroy in a way that he'd never seen her do with any other man.

"Okay, let's stay quiet and listen," Noah said with an ear peeled.

"*Nee*, they don't seem like serial killers," Catherine said as she rolled her eyes before looking at a bag in Esther's hand.

"*Ach*." Esther handed the bag to Catherine. "It's a gift, just a few baked goods that we brought over." She cut her eyes at her sister. "Just in case Lizzie didn't hear *Gott* correctly, let this be our apology."

Noah had to stifle laughter again. "Those ladies are funny," he whispered to Ruth and Leroy.

"*Danki*," Catherine said. "Do you want to stay for a while?"

Esther shook her head. "*Nee*, but how is your *mammi* doing?"

Catherine shrugged. "It depends on the day. She is okay right now, just napping."

"You give her our *lieb*," Esther said.

"And let us know how this all pans out with you and Noah, and with Ruth and Leroy." Lizzie pressed her palms together. "You're going to end up married, Catherine Lapp."

Noah envisioned himself as Catherine's husband. It was a crazy thought after knowing her for such a short time. Under different circumstances, he would move in and help her take care of her grandmother, but he could never leave his family, especially his father who relied on him so much. If God really told Lizzie that he and Catherine would be a good match, then why not make it a doable situation?

Ruth went and shuffled some dishes around on the table, the way Leroy had done earlier.

"We should probably stop spying and actually clean this up." Noah forced himself to move away from the doorway, then carried a stack of dishes to the counter.

Ruth and Leroy began to help him clean, too, and he heard Catherine telling Lizzie and Esther goodbye.

"The owners of The Peony Inn brought these goodies for us," Catherine said as she walked into the kitchen and lifted the bag in her hand before she set it on the table and sighed. "Please stop cleaning the kitchen. You shouldn't be doing that."

Ruth laughed. "You're right—about the men. Noah has never washed a dish in his life, and Leroy, I don't know about you, but I suspect you aren't handy in the kitchen either. You two will just slow us down." She turned to Catherine, then back to Noah and Leroy. "We've got this. Be scarce." She shooed the men with her hand.

Noah shrugged, but he found it hard to leave the room. Would Ruth insist that they leave early the next morning to go to Fannie and Amos's house, or would they be able to squeeze in one more day here?

It was warm enough for Noah and Leroy to retreat to the porch without coats. As sunrays beamed beneath the rafters of the porch, pulling in rays of orange and yellow hues, Noah cast his eyes toward a cluster of trees in the distance. The re-emergence of fall peeked out from branches shedding snow and being replaced by red and orange leaves.

"Do you think you'll keep in contact with Ruth after we're gone?" Noah tipped back the rim of his hat as he looped his thumbs beneath his suspenders.

"I sure hope so."

Noah sighed. "I don't want to leave tomorrow."

"So, don't."

Noah looked at Leroy in the rocking chair next to him.

"You can be home in a day, *ya*? Not too far from here. I guess it would be easy for you to stay."

"I'd have no motive to stay if Ruth leaves."

Somehow, Noah needed to hear that. He was pretty sure Leroy only had eyes for Ruth, but it was comforting to hear him say it.

"You never said if you had plans for Thanksgiving. Do you have a family who missed you for the holiday?" Noah felt badly that he hadn't inquired about Leroy's situation earlier. If Ruth had, his sister hadn't mentioned it.

"I did, but like you, I have a large family. I'm not going to say I wasn't missed." He shrugged. "But I wasn't missed all that much." Smiling, he said, "I preferred to celebrate here for the obvious reasons.

Noah understood perfectly.

It was late in the afternoon, after devotions, when Leroy asked Ruth to go for a walk, leaving Catherine and Noah in the living room with Catherine's grandmother. She had come downstairs after her nap.

"*Mammi*, I'm sorry Jessica didn't show up today," Catherine said as her grandmother stood staring out the window. She'd wondered all day if her grandmother would revert to thinking that Catherine was Jessica, but she'd stayed on course, frequently looking out the window.

"I don't understand." Her grandmother's voice was shaky as she spoke. "I'm sure I gave her the right address."

Catherine glanced at Noah before she turned to her

grandmother. "*Mammi*, when did you talk to Jessica? Did you write to her?"

When her grandmother stayed on course for this long, it was hard for Catherine not to picture Jessica as a real person.

"She wrote to me." Her grandmother sat on the couch. "I don't know how long ago."

Noah sat in the rocking chair while Catherine took a seat next to her grandmother. "Did you write her back?"

"*Ya*, of course. I invited her for Thanksgiving. She told me she would be here in time for the noon meal." Her grandmother lowered her head.

"Maybe she got sick," Catherine said.

"Who?" Her grandmother raised an eyebrow.

"Jessica. Maybe that's why she couldn't make it for Thanksgiving."

Her grandmother huffed before she stood up. "I don't know a Jessica," she said as she walked toward her bedroom.

Noah gave Catherine a much-needed hug when her grandmother was out of sight.

"I was starting to believe that there actually was a Jessica." She eased out of his arms. "She stuck to the same story for such a long time, and now she's changed again." She shook her head. "It's so hard to see her going back and forth like this. The worst part is that we can have a normal conversation when she seems to know and understand everything, but she might not remember any of it the next day."

"I wish there was something I could do." He kissed her

on the forehead, and the feel of his lips against her skin was something she could get used to.

"Just having company for Thanksgiving was wonderful. I-I fight bitterness toward *mei* parents, especially during the holidays. I try to remember that *Gott* has a plan, but it's hard to always keep the faith." She gazed into his eyes. "I've enjoyed having you here, Noah."

"I don't want to leave you," he said as sadness crept into his voice.

Catherine wanted to say, "then don't," but Noah likely had a full life at home, with no desire to relocate over a crush he might have on her. She swallowed back an urge to respond.

He was quiet. Was he waiting for her to ask him to stay in town? Even if he didn't have commitments at home, Catherine's grandmother could be a handful.

"Maybe . . ." Noah paused. ". . . maybe you would consider coming to Pennsylvania for a visit? Have you ever been there?"

Catherine relished the thought of visiting Noah and seeing a new place. "*Nee*, I haven't. I've heard Lancaster County is beautiful."

He smiled. "It is, although we are not right in the middle of the touristy area. We have a hundred acres right outside of Paradise."

Paradise. Catherine allowed herself to envision a visit, knowing it was impossible. She couldn't leave her grandmother. "It sounds lovely."

Noah nodded, his lips pressed together as if he knew she couldn't visit. "It is." He paused again. "Today was a wonderful Thanksgiving."

Catherine couldn't have agreed more, except for one thing. "It was for me, but I wish *Mammi* hadn't been so disappointed."

Noah hung his head for a few moments before he looked up at her. "She won't get better, will she?"

Catherine was pretty sure she'd told him that, but she shook her head and whispered, "*Nee,* she won't." She wanted to change the subject, but every route seemed to lead back to her and Noah not together. She wanted to carry on with the dream as long as she could. "Lizzie and Esther wanted to know if their matchmaking efforts had paid off." She tried to chuckle and keep it light, but hearing her own voice, she didn't think she had done well.

Noah grinned. "I'd have to say that Leroy and Ruth seem smitten." He cupped her cheeks and gazed into her eyes. "And I can certainly say the same about my growing feelings for you."

Catherine felt herself blushing, but she wanted her true thoughts out there. "Why do you think *Gott* would put us all on a path that has nowhere to go?"

Noah looked in her eyes for a long few seconds. "Maybe it does." He kissed her softly on the lips until Catherine almost swooned.

"I don't see how," she said before Noah kissed her again, this time leaving her weak in the knees and with a growing frustration regarding God.

"Someone's here." Noah stepped back from Catherine. "I hear footsteps on the porch."

Catherine went to the door, eased it open, and through the screen, she saw Leroy, Ruth, and someone she didn't

AN AMISH THANKSGIVING (A ROMANCE)

know. A woman, maybe her mother's age or a little older, stood next to them. She wore a tan pantsuit and had short brown hair speckled with gray. Her makeup was modest, but when she smiled, her eyes twinkled. She carried a small suitcase with her and had a brown purse hung on her shoulder.

"Hello," Catherine said as Leroy opened the screen door to let the women enter the den.

Catherine closed the door, fearing Lizzie and Esther had sent another person to stay. Not only was there not a suitable candidate for this woman—if that was the sisters' plan—but Catherine was out of rooms for another house guest.

"While we were walking, we found this woman shivering alongside the road." Ruth gleamed as she spoke. "A cab dropped her off at the wrong place."

Catherine stifled a big sigh. Didn't Ruth realize they didn't have room for any more overnight guests? Catherine forced a smile before she looked at the woman. "I'm afraid we have a full *haus*, but I'm sure The Peony Inn has rooms available. I can confirm that, if you'd like. And, if they are full . . ." Catherine doubted it. ". . . there are several other bed and breakfasts in the area."

The woman, still shivering, said, "I'm looking for someone, Mary Marie Byler" She glanced at Ruth, then Leroy. "This couple said she lived here."

Catherine tipped her head slightly to one side, guarded, but curious. "And you are?"

The woman clutched her small brown purse to her chest, her suitcase on the floor beside her. "Am I mistaken? If I have the wrong address, I'm happy to find other accommodations."

Ruth cleared her throat. "Catherine . . ." She nodded to the stranger. "This woman's name is Jessica."

CHAPTER 13

*C*atherine's jaw dropped, and her first thought was that her grandmother had a pen pal named Jessica and had invited this woman to visit.

"Did *mei grandmammi* write you a letter?"

The woman dropped one arm, the other one clutching her purse. "I wrote to her first." She put a hand to her chest and gasped. "Are you Catherine?"

"*Ya*," Catherine said cautiously, not at all prepared when the woman threw her arms around her, squeezed her tightly, then eased away still grasping her arms. "You look exactly like your mother."

Catherine didn't even like to think about her mother, nor did she want to be compared to her in any way. "*Mei mudder* doesn't live here."

"Yes, that's what Mary Marie said in her letter, and you are as beautiful as I imagined you would be." The woman finally released Catherine's arms, probably because Catherine was clenching her teeth and stood as rigid as a mannequin in one of the English boutiques.

"Forgive me." The woman shook her head before she spoke. "I'm Jessica, Mary Marie's sister."

Catherine frowned as she took a step backward. "*Mei mammi* doesn't have a *schweschder*." She glanced at Noah, then Leroy and Ruth, before she narrowed her eyebrows at this stranger. "There must be a mistake."

They all turned around when someone coughed. It was Catherine's grandmother entering the den as she rubbed her eyes. When she finally looked up, tears formed in the corners of her eyes, and she ran to the woman who called herself Jessica.

"It *is* you." Her grandmother pulled the woman into an embrace and sobbed. "I thought you weren't coming."

"I'm so sorry, Mary Marie." The woman cried hard also. "My flight was late arriving, and then the taxi driver dropped me at a house down the road."

"That *haus* down the road is abandoned," Catherine said softly as she took in the scene before her while she pressed a hand to her chest, her heart beating wildly.

"I've missed you all these years," her grandmother said through tears before she finally eased away and looked at Catherine. "This is *mei* baby *schweschder*."

Catherine knew her eyes were round as saucers. "*Mammi*, you don't have a *schweschder*."

"I never spoke of her. Back then, when a person was shunned, they were never to be talked about again," her grandmother said. "The *Ordnung* has become more forgiving, and I did speak with the bishop about this before I contacted her."

Catherine was too stunned to move. When did her grandmother speak to the bishop? Then, she recalled a visit from him last month. Catherine had left the room to run a load of clothes through the wringer when her grandmother had asked to speak to the bishop privately.

"So, you were shunned?" she asked the woman. *It must run in the family.* "Why are you here now?" She heard her accusatory voice and was tempted to say that they didn't have any money if that's what the woman was thinking.

"Let's all sit," her grandmother said as she motioned for Jessica to join her on the couch. Ruth took the far end of the couch on the other side of Catherine's grandmother. Leroy sat in one of the rocking chairs. Noah stayed standing beside Catherine.

Her grandmother, holding tight to Jessica's hand, looked up at Catherine, tears still spilling from her eyes. She swiped the moisture from her face, then took a deep breath. "I'm sixteen years older than Jessica. When she turned seventeen, she left our community, and she'd already been baptized, so therefore she was shunned. It broke *mei* heart into a million pieces." She glanced at Jessica and smiled. "I was already married when she left, but she's *mei* only sibling, and we haven't seen each other since she left."

"But I have been home," Jessica said with her chin tucked, wiping at her own tears before she locked eyes with Catherine's grandmother. "I came home for Mom and Dad's funeral. I just stayed in the background. I didn't know how to approach you, and I was afraid you would get in trouble for speaking to me. But when you wrote and said you had gotten permission from the bishop for me to visit, I got here as quickly as I could."

Her grandmother grasped both of Jessica's hands. "I

want to hear everything. Did you marry? Do you have *kinner*? Are you happy?"

Catherine felt like an intruder listening in on a huge chunk of her life that she'd never known existed.

"I was married for forty-two years. Phil was a wonderful man, but we were never blessed with children." She gazed into Catherine's grandmother's eyes. "I have led a good and Christ-filled life. I might have left here, but my faith never left me." She shook her head. "I was young and didn't know what I wanted. There was a time when I wanted to come home, but I didn't know how. I met Phil at a church retreat while I was staying at friend's house." She shrugged. "It was meant to be, and we married when I turned nineteen."

"*Ach*, Jessica." Her grandmother had all her wits about her, and Catherine silently prayed that God would give her this time and that she would remember it all tomorrow. And the next day . . . and the next day. "You should have brought Phil with you."

Jessica dabbed at her eyes again. "I'm afraid he passed on two months ago. I have been wallowing in grief. I didn't leave the house for a month." She smiled slightly. "Then I got the courage to write you, Mary Marie, and that bravery could have only been orchestrated by God. I knew I had to see you."

Catherine sat in the empty rocking chair, barely able to contain her emotions, her lip trembling. But how would Jessica feel tomorrow if her grandmother had no recollection of this conversation, or possibly, didn't even know who Jessica was?

"I'm so sorry I missed Thanksgiving at noon." She

hugged Catherine's grandmother again, such sadness in her voice.

Ruth looked at Catherine just as she looked at her, and they smiled. "We have an abundance of leftovers," Catherine said as she got to her feet and pressed her palms together. "I say we recreate the moment."

"Oh, no, please don't go to that trouble." Jessica shook her head.

"I would *lieb* to help Catherine get the meal on the table," Ruth added. "We have so much to be grateful for that it seems to warrant a second Thanksgiving." She smiled brighter. "We always have a second Christmas, so maybe this will be a new tradition for your family—Second Thanksgiving." She turned to Catherine. "What do you think?"

Catherine was still in shock, but she nodded. "*Ya*, I think that's a lovely idea."

"That would be a dream come true," Jessica said, wiping more tears from her eyes.

"I will help the *maeds* get everything ready," Catherine's grandmother said as she stood.

"*Mammi, nee*." Catherine spoke with a lingering tremble in her voice. "Ruth and I can handle this. You and your *schweschder* take this time to catch up."

Catherine barely made it to the kitchen before she leaned against the wall, put a hand across her stomach, and let the tears spill.

When she opened her eyes, Noah was standing beside her.

"*Mammi* won't remember all this. I know it. As wonderful as it is to have Jessica here, I'm afraid it will break the woman's heart when *Mammi* doesn't recognize her. And it could even happen in the middle of the meal." She gazed into Noah's eyes. "It breaks *mei* heart every time she doesn't know me. You would think I'd get used to it, but it always hurts."

He cupped her cheek. "But I know you also cherish the time when she does know you. You must give this to *Gott*. Your *mammi's* sister showing up is clearly an emotional and welcomed event for them. All you can do is make it the most it can be, and you have three new friends who can help you."

As Catherine gazed into his eyes, she prayed that he would be able to stay, but he'd already told her how important he was to his father's business. It would be unfair for her to make him choose. Besides, they really didn't know each other after only a few days. Still, it felt like much longer.

"Are-are you and Ruth leaving tomorrow?" She chewed her bottom lip and avoided his eyes.

"I think we have to," Noah said before he put his finger beneath her chin and tilted it upward, lifting her eyes to his. "But I don't want to."

Again, Catherine questioned God's path for her. This was the first man to come along who she could see herself dating, possibly even in a long-term relationship. It was hard not to be angry with the Lord.

"Will you write to me?" Catherine met his gaze as his lips brushed against hers.

"I would like that very much." He kissed her again. "I'm so happy for your *grandmammi* and her *schweschder*, and I understand your concerns, but all the worry in the world won't change anything. Leave that for *Gott*. And if you're all right now, I think I'll go help Leroy tend to his horse."

She nodded, and when he was gone, she squeezed her eyes closed. Gott, *please spare* mei *heart. This is someone I could* lieb.

After her prayer, she peeked her head around the corner. Ruth was walking her way. Her grandmother and Catherine's newly found great-aunt were still clasping hands. *What a reunion it must be for both.*

"I was just giving you and Noah a moment alone," Ruth whispered as she sidled up to Catherine. "After all these years. It's beautiful, isn't it?" She stretched her neck to see into the living room.

Catherine did the same and couldn't take her eyes from the two sisters who hadn't seen each other in decades.

She needed to put her worries aside and rejoice for her grandmother and Jessica, but she would still pray that things didn't go sour for either woman, and that one—or both—of the sisters weren't left with a broken heart.

Catherine's own heart would surely be breaking tomorrow when Noah and Ruth left.

CHAPTER 14

*N*oah forced himself to eat a second meal, which normally wouldn't be a problem, but the thought of leaving Catherine the following morning tugged at his heart. He wondered if Ruth felt the same way about leaving Leroy, but he hadn't had a chance to talk to her privately. He tried to stay focused on the conversation between Mary Marie and her sister, Jessica.

"Remember when *Daed* used to make moonshine in the basement?" Catherine's grandmother asked, chuckling afterward.

Jessica laughed. "I sure do. I also remember getting caught down there doing taste tests with my friends."

"*Ach*," Mary Marie said. "I remember that. You all ran!"

Both women laughed, which was nice to hear, but Noah was still plagued with thoughts of his departure.

Mary Marie scooted back her chair, stood, then shuffled to the refrigerator. She returned with a bottle of ketchup. Noah couldn't imagine what she needed ketchup for since they were having the same Thanksgiving supper that they had for the noon meal.

When Catherine's grandmother began to squirt an abundant amount of ketchup atop everything on her plate—turkey, dressing, corn, and peas--Noah glanced at Catherine, who appeared to be holding her breath.

~

"MAMMI, do you really want that much ketchup on your plate?" Catherine asked cautiously, fearing Jessica was about to get a taste of life with Catherine's grandmother.

"*Nee*, I don't want ketchup." Her grandmother frowned, then her eyes welled with tears. "I've ruined *mei* meal." She covered her face with her hands.

Catherine looked at Jessica, who had stopped eating, her mouth gaping open. If Catherine had known Jessica was coming, she could have warned her.

"*Mammi*, I will prepare you another plate." Catherine stood, though as she went to pick up her grandmother's ketchup-drenched food, her grandmother slapped her hand away. "Jessica stop. I'm perfectly capable of choosing *mei* own food."

And that was how quickly her grandmother could shift. Catherine returned to her seat and glanced at Jessica, who was still focused on her sister.

"This turkey and dressing are delicious," Jessica finally said after clearing her throat. "I appreciate you all reheating everything for this second Thanksgiving. I'm very grateful."

"We're happy to have you here, and it was no trouble

getting everything out again." Catherine admired the way Jessica carried the conversation despite the mishap.

"I *lieb* to eat, especially this kind of food." Leroy grinned, then winked at Ruth. "I like this second Thanksgiving, a new tradition."

Catherine's guests fell into sync by carrying on the conversation as if nothing out of the ordinary had happened. *What a blessing.* Catherine wondered what Leroy and Ruth talked about on their walk. Had their feelings progressed in the way that Catherine's had for Noah, and seemingly the way Noah felt about her? Catherine's stomach churned again at the thought of him leaving. Ruth would leave also. And she'd be alone with her grandmother again. She briefly wondered where Jessica would sleep tonight. She didn't have any bedrooms left.

"*Wie bischt,*" Catherine's grandmother said to Jessica. "I don't believe we've met."

Catherine took a deep breath and opened her mouth to say something, but when she hesitated, Jessica said, "I'm Jessica." Then she smiled. There was an air of sympathy in her eyes, but not pity, and Catherine appreciated that. She'd learned to recognize the difference.

Her grandmother dabbed her mouth with her napkin, then stared for a long time at her sister. "Jessica, I need to excuse myself."

"Sure, that's fine." Jessica smiled again.

After her grandmother was out of earshot and almost to her downstairs bedroom, Catherine turned to Jessica . . . her great aunt. "If I had known you were coming, I could have warned you."

"How long have you and your husband been tending to Mary Marie?" She nodded toward Noah, then refocused on Catherine.

"Uh . . . *nee*, he isn't *mei* husband." She felt a blush creeping into her cheeks, and she couldn't bring herself to look at Noah, until he spoke.

"Not yet," he said through a bold grin.

Catherine couldn't help but smile. *If only it could be so. Did love at first sight exist?*

"I knew I saw a spark between the two of you." Jessica waited for an answer.

"*Mammi* started to get this way about around the time *Mamm* and *Daed* left to get an *Englisch* divorce, which was four years ago. The doctor doesn't think it's related." Catherine hung her head and sighed. "I'm so sorry this happened while you are here, but she rarely goes twenty-four hours without some sort of episode."

"Please don't apologize. And you and Mary Marie must have been devastated when your parents chose that route."

Catherine nodded. "*Ya*. I hear from *mei mudder* sometimes, but . . ." She didn't want to overshare, fearful the bitterness in her heart would spill out of her mouth. "*Mammi* has dementia. Some days, she does really *gut*, but other days, it's a challenge. She might not remember you tomorrow, or the conversation you had." Catherine paused. "It's funny because *Mammi* has mentioned moonshine over the past couple of years. I usually make her some dark-colored tea, and she drinks it as if it really is moonshine."

"We never drank alcohol, except that one time when I

got caught with my friends. Mary Marie made light about that." Jessica pressed her lips together and looked somewhere over Catherine's shoulder. "Maybe she didn't know how much trouble I got in over that little escapade." She paused, still with a faraway look in her eyes. "Our father was not always a kind man."

Catherine had never known her great-grandparents, nor had her grandmother spoken of them very much, only about the moonshine in the basement. "I didn't know that," Catherine said. "*Mammi* didn't talk about them, and they had passed by the time I was born."

"I choose not to look back too much. As I told Mary Marie, I did attend both their funerals, but I otherwise did not keep in contact with them, or sadly, with my sister." She paused. "I was hoping to make up for a little of the time we lost."

"I hope you are able to do so and that she will remember," Catherine said as she tried to sound hopeful.

"I'll take whatever I can get," Jessica said. "But I'm not going to trouble you by staying here since you didn't even know I was coming. I'm sure I can find accommodations nearby."

Catherine felt a wave of relief wash over her since she didn't have any extra bedrooms, but she didn't want Jessica to feel unwelcome. "I-I, uh . . ."

"I'm leaving shortly," Leroy said, glancing at Ruth briefly. "*Mei* room will be available if . . ."

Catherine quickly snuck a look at Ruth, but the woman didn't react at all. "Jessica, in that case, I'd *lieb* for you to stay with us, but I'd understand if you don't want to. *Mammi* has *gut* days and bad days, sometimes her mood shifts within hours, as you saw earlier."

"I don't want to put you out, but I would like to stay to get to know my sister better. And, hopefully, I can be a help to you, not a hinderance."

Catherine tried to envision a day out shopping or eating out with a friend without having to worry about her grandmother. She suspected Jessica would tire of the daily strength it took to take care of her grandmother.

"You're welcome for as long as you would like." Catherine glanced at Ruth again, but still no reaction to the news that Leroy would be leaving today. *Hmm . . .*

NOAH COULD USUALLY READ his sister's expressions, but when Ruth didn't react to Leroy's announcement, he worried she was taking his departure hard. They'd presumably parted ways privately. He waited until much later in the evening, after Leroy had said his goodbyes to everyone else, before he knocked on Ruth's door. "It's me."

"Come in." Ruth sat on the side of her bed folding dresses that had previously been hung on the rack on the wall, leaving one still hanging.

"I guess we're leaving in the morning." Noah swallowed back a lump in his throat at the thought of leaving Catherine.

"*You* are." She raised an eyebrow as she challenged him with her response.

"What does that mean?" Noah folded his arms across his chest.

"It means that I will be staying at The Peony Inn. I've already spoken to Lizzie, and they are giving me a ridiculously low rental rate, by the week."

Noah's jaw dropped. "You can't do that."

"I can and I am. I've already spoken to *Mamm* too. She wasn't happy, but she understands." Ruth went back to folding her clothes.

"This is because of Leroy." Noah heard the harshness in his voice, but he felt betrayed. And jealous.

"*Ya*, it is."

"You can't just give up your life for a man you barely know," Noah said, scowling at her.

"Why not? What is keeping me in Pennsylvania?"

Noah grunted. "Uh, your family? Our parents . . . siblings." He shrugged. "You've let a man sway you into staying here without considering the consequences. You're being irresponsible." This wasn't like his sister at all. But it did explain Leroy's cheerful disposition when he'd left.

Ruth pinched her lips together and gave him a fake smile, one he'd seen plenty of times. "You can call me irresponsible if you'd like, but I'm a twenty-seven-year-old woman who can choose to do what she wants."

Noah's jaw dropped. "But why would you overhaul your life like this? What if it doesn't work out?" Again, jealousy crept into his emotions, wishing he could stay, also, to see if things would work out with him and Catherine. "What about your friends? Your quilting parties? How can you give up all of that so easily?"

"I never said it would be easy." She snapped her suitcase closed. "All I can say is that I've never felt the way I

BETH WISEMAN

feel when I'm with Leroy. I owe it to myself to find out if what I'm feeling is real." She sighed. "Noah, I know you feel loyalty to *Daed*, and *ya*, he would be angry if you chose not to return, but don't you want to know if Catherine is the person for you? We've both dated plenty of people. And I hate to point out the obvious, but we're not getting any younger. I want to start a family. I know you want those things, too, and I've seen you with Catherine. It's more than a spark."

Noah lowered his arms and sighed. "*Ya*, there does seem to be something there." He couldn't imagine leaving her, but he couldn't imagine staying either.

Ruth stood, walked to him, and kissed him on the cheek. "Go pray about it, Noah. *Gott* will lead you in the right direction."

"I don't know about that," he grumbled before he left her room and went down the hallway. Inside his room, he sat on the bed, his heart a tornado of emotions.

But he knew what he was going to do.

CHAPTER 15

*T*he next morning, the start of breakfast was uneventful, but with luggage stacked by the door, Catherine tried to prepare herself to say goodbye to Noah and Ruth. Then she'd be left with a great aunt she didn't know and her grandmother. She'd do anything for the woman she had cared for over the past four years, but she suspected Jessica would stay a couple of days, then leave. Amid all those thoughts, was Noah. She'd allowed herself to get attached to someone she couldn't be with.

Ruth tapped a spoon to her glass filled with orange juice. The empty seat at the table reminded them of Leroy's departure the night before. "I have an announcement to make." She glanced around the table at Catherine, Jessica, Noah, and Catherine's grandmother. "I've had a wonderful time here." She smiled. "And I've decided to extend my stay. I've rented a room at The Peony Inn on a weekly basis." She rolled her eyes, still grinning. "All of a sudden they have plenty of rooms." Ruth looked at

Catherine. "So, I won't be going home to Pennsylvania, at least not right away. I'll be traveling to visit our relatives whom we missed at Thanksgiving dinner, but I'll be returning to The Peony Inn." She smiled again. "I like this area. And, Catherine, I'd *lieb* to stop by often and help with whatever you might need."

Catherine's insides swirled as her eyes darted in Noah's direction, asking him the silent question. *Are you staying too?* But the man of her dreams lowered his head.

"You're staying because of that fellow who was here." Her grandmother tugged on her ear. "What was his name?"

"Leroy," Catherine said as she laid a hand across her stomach, willing her nerves to settle.

"*Ya*, Leroy." Her grandmother smiled, then looked at Noah. Catherine was grateful that she remembered Jessica this morning, and mostly everyone else, but she feared what her grandmother was about to ask Noah. Even though Catherine had a burning desire to know if he'd made the same decision as his sister. "And what about you, young man?" Her grandmother lifted both her eyebrows. "Will you be traveling to see your family and staying at The Peony Inn too?"

Catherine wasn't sure if her grandmother had forgotten Noah's name or not, and it didn't really matter, she supposed. But now the question was out there, and Catherine's heart sank when he shook his head.

"*Nee*, I have a driver picking me up this morning. I'll briefly visit with *mei* relatives before heading to the bus station, but then I'm headed home I'm needed back at work." He looked at Catherine. "I've enjoyed *mei* stay here."

She wanted to scream at him. What about all the hand holding and making out like teenagers? Maybe Catherine had just been a fun playmate while he was here. But she couldn't deny that she'd enjoyed his company also. And she'd known that she was playing with fire, that Noah wasn't staying. She'd known that from the beginning. But Ruth hadn't planned to extend her stay . . . until she met Leroy.

When her eyes began to get moist, she stood. "Excuse me, please."

She rushed out of the kitchen, then out the door in the living room, and stood on the porch eyeing the clear blue sky with only scattered remnants of dirty white snow left lingering between brown sprouts of dead grass. The weather was fit for travel, for sure. She turned when the door closed behind her, and she told herself she would not beg Noah to stay. But it was Ruth who joined her on the porch.

"I know that Noah wants to stay and get to know you better, Catherine, but he is worried about upsetting our *daed* since Noah is second in command at the company our family owns." She paused. "And I'm not sure if this will make you feel better or worse, but I've never seen him look at anyone the way he looks at you."

Catherine put a hand across her stomach again as she stifled tears. "I understand. I would never expect him to stay here. Even if it wasn't due to his job, *mei mammi* can be a handful. So *mei* time is not *mei* own." Not wanting to give the wrong impression, she added, "But I don't mind tending to her."

Ruth put a hand on her arm. "Your great-aunt is here now, and I'll be coming by to help also." Sighing, she said, "Catherine, *Gott* has a way of working things out. I told Noah to pray about this. Just because he's leaving now doesn't mean that it is the end of what might have been blooming." She paused, twisted her mouth from one side to the other. "It might be selfish of me to stay, but Leroy and I discussed it, and we believe there is something between us worth pursuing."

"I'm happy for you." Catherine tried to sound excited for her new friend, even forcing a smile. "Leroy seems like a nice man."

"And handsome." Ruth winked at her. "But don't you give up on Noah."

Catherine tried to smile again, but what choice did she have but to give up on him? Noah couldn't stay here, and she couldn't leave.

When she heard dishes clanking from in the kitchen, she assumed her grandmother and great aunt were cleaning the kitchen. "I should go in," she told Ruth.

Ruth nodded. Catherine saw the sympathy in her eyes.

NOAH TOLD Mary Marie and Jessica goodbye. Ruth had already left. Now, it was time for him to say goodbye to Catherine, a reality that shot a pang of remorse coursing through his veins and straight to his heart.

She followed him onto the porch. His car would be arriving any minute.

"I wish I could stay, Catherine." He cupped her cheeks and gazed into her eyes, hoping she could see and feel how much he meant it.

"I understand," she said in a shaky voice as she stepped back a little. "I've enjoyed our time together." Her voice sounded formal. Noah understood. She was trying to distance herself from him.

"I'll write to you if that's all right."

She nodded. "I'd like that."

He reached for her hand and squeezed, willing her not to pull away. "And I'll be praying for you, your *mammi*, and your great aunt."

"*Danki.*"

Noah heard car tires crunching against gravel in the distance. He didn't have much time.

"Catherine," he said breathless as he pulled her into his arms and kissed her with all the tenderness he felt in his heart. He kept kissing her until the car was in the driveway.

He drew both her hands to his mouth and kissed them tenderly before giving her one last kiss on the cheek before he picked up his suitcase and walked to the car.

The driver, a tall fellow with white hair, took his suitcase and put it in the trunk. Noah climbed into the backseat and kept his head down. If he looked up at her, he might not be able to leave. And he knew he had to go.

~

When Catherine walked back into the house, her grandmother and great-aunt were on the couch, twisted so they were facing each other and holding hands.

"Mary Marie was just telling me about your parents, what happened with them." Jessica shook her head. "She said you rarely hear from your mother, and your father doesn't correspond at all?"

Jessica posed the statement more as a question, probably wondering if Catherine's grandmother was telling the truth. "Sadly, that's true."

"We can't focus on a decision we have no control over." Her grandmother shook her head, then smiled. "But we can be thankful that the Lord saw fit for me to be reunited with *mei* sister."

Catherine didn't think a change of subject would shift her gloominess, but she'd had a question for her great aunt since she had arrived. "Jessica isn't a common Amish name. I don't know anyone with that name, and I can't recall ever seeing it in *The Budget* newspaper." She tipped her head to one side, pondering the name chosen by her great-grandparents.

"I remember when I was old enough to realize I didn't know any other Jessicas either, I asked my mother. She said it was of Hebrew origin, gave me a lengthy explanation about its mention in the Bible, but it basically means 'God beholds'." She smiled. "I guess it never caught on in any Amish communities."

Catherine nodded. "I just wondered." She tried to smile, her thoughts drifting farther and farther away from this conversation.

She listened to the two women playing catch-up on

their entire lives. They spoke about when they married and the lives they had led. They also shared more emotional things, like how Catherine's grandfather had died a young man from a rare type of cancer and how sweet they both thought it was that Ruth was going to stay in Montgomery to see if there was truly a romance growing between her and Leroy.

Catherine was happy that her grandmother was staying on track, at least for now. How would Jessica feel if she had to reenact this entire conversation again tomorrow? It was exhausting, and even though Catherine longed for a break sometimes, she'd never leave her grandmother, not even for Noah. She suspected they would write a few times here and there, but distance would only make any romantic opportunity grow farther away.

Her heart was heavy, and she hadn't slept well last night, causing a series of yawns she was unable to stifle.

"Catherine, your grandmother and I have so much to catch up on, and I can see how exhausted you are," Jessica said. "Why don't you go lay down and rest?"

Nothing had ever sounded so good. Catherine wanted to bury her head in her pillow and cry. Her chest hurt from holding in tears all day. "But . . ." She glanced at her grandmother before she looked back at Jessica. "What if—"

"We will be fine," Jessica locked eyes with her. "It's okay."

It probably wouldn't be, but Catherine wanted to lament in private. She pointed to her bedroom. "I'll just be right over there if you need me."

Her great-aunt nodded. *Aunt.* A woman she never knew existed.

Catherine shuffled to her bedroom, prepared to fall face-first into her pillow, but something caught her eye. An envelope in the middle of the bed had her name written on it.

CHAPTER 16

*C*atherine stared at the envelope for a few moments, suspecting it was from Noah, but she didn't even know his handwriting. Maybe it was from Ruth.

She peeled back the flap and opened the envelope.

Dear Catherine,

There were so many things I wanted to say to you before I left. At mei *age, I've courted plenty of women. That's not to say that I went wild about it.*

Catherine grinned.

No one has touched mei *heart the way you have, especially in such a short time frame. I have been fighting the urge to be angry at* Gott *for putting someone who seems so perfectly suited to me—and beautiful—only to make it seem like an impossible situation.*

But I don't believe in impossible situations. So, I am choosing to believe that Gott *has a plan for us. We just don't know what it is.*

By the time you read this letter, I will be gone and missing you already.

You will be constantly in mei *prayers . . . you, your* grand-mammi *and your great-aunt.*

Yours most truly,

Noah

Catherine reread the letter two more times before she placed it in the drawer of her nightstand. She buried her face in her pillow, as she had planned, then let the tears come rolling out like a waterspout that had been unplugged, dampening her pillow until she felt her swollen eyes beginning to give up the fight. There were no more tears left. Her life would return to normal, albeit her great aunt was here.

When she sat up, she let that sink in for a few moments. Maybe she would be able to go to the grocery store on her own. Perhaps, she could have lunch with friends, those she used to have, who were all married and raising families now. Even if their schedules allowed for a quick visit, how refreshing that would be.

Sighing, she rolled onto her back and stared at the ceiling, a cow mooing in the distance, and her chickens squawking in the barn. Tomorrow was a new day, and she needed to embrace it and not lose hope for the future. *Easier said than done.* Maybe she could enjoy these occasional naps while Jessica was here. For however short a time that might be.

It was after midnight when Noah arrived at home. His parents and siblings were always asleep by ten, so he was surprised to see his mother sitting on the couch with a lit lantern on the coffee table.

"What are you doing up, *Mamm*?"

His mother was in a white robe with her graying hair in a bun atop her head. "I just couldn't sleep," she said, sounding defeated.

"You're upset about Ruth staying, *ya*?" Noah set down his suitcase and sat beside her on the couch.

"*Ya*, I am." His mother sighed again. "Out of all *mei maeds*, your twin *schweschder* is the most logical. She's strong, confident, and her moves are almost always calculated. This just isn't like her."

Noah couldn't really argue, but he'd seen the way Leroy and his eldest sister looked at each other, the way they interacted. It might have been out of character for Ruth, but he'd witnessed it. "*Mamm*, I know you want all of us to be happy, and Leroy seems to make Ruth happy. Don't you think she deserves a chance to see if she's met the person *Gott* chose for her?" *And why am I undeserving of that same opportunity?*

His mother clasped her hands in her lap and was quiet before she turned to Noah. "Ruth called and told me that you also found a woman you are interested in." She shook her head. "How did that happen in such a small town as Montgomery, Indiana?"

Noah realized they were all abusing their cell phones, but when travel was involved, it felt mandatory. "I don't know, *Mamm*, but I knew I had to come home. *Daed* would have trouble running the business without me."

She smiled slightly. "That's what happens when you are the only *sohn* among a gaggle of women." His mother locked eyes with him. "It must seem incredibly unfair that Ruth has an opportunity to pursue a *lieb* interest and you don't."

Noah wondered if his mother would put in a good word with his father. Maybe he could arrange for another trip to Indiana soon. He respected his father too much to carry the thought any farther. "I understand that he needs me here."

He held his breath, clinging to the hope that his mother would help him even though he was a grown man who technically could do whatever he wanted. Folks pressured women his age to marry, but men seemed to be given a pass even when they aged out of the dating pool.

His mother reached for his hand. "I wish I could tell you that your father didn't need you, but his jobs and income dropped just in the short time you were gone." She paused, tipped her head to one side. "Is there any chance that this woman you took an interest in would be willing to come here for a visit?"

"*Nee*. Her *grandmammi* has dementia and can't be left alone." Noah swallowed hard as Catherine's face flashed in his mind's eye, etching her sweet smile into his head to revisit later. He'd never find someone like her. He was sure of it. Did his mother see it in his eyes?

"Sometimes, life is just unfair, and I'm sorry, *sohn*." She stood, yawning.

Noah rose slowly, exhausted from travel and feeling the hopelessness settle around his heart. "Goodnight, *Mamm*." He kissed her on the forehead before he lifted his suitcase and trudged upstairs. Maybe getting back into his routine would ease the pain in his heart about not seeing Catherine. He recalled the hope he'd conveyed in his letter to Catherine, how he didn't believe in hopeless situations. Normally, Noah was a 'cup half full' type of person. But now, his cup was emptier than it had ever been.

CATHERINE AWOKE from her nap when she heard her grandmother screeching like a wounded owl. She ran barefoot out of the bedroom, her heart pounding against her chest.

When she entered the living room, Jessica was standing in the middle of the rug with her arms around Catherine's grandmother.

"You're all right, Mary Marie. I'm here now. I'm not going anywhere. I will take care of you." Jessica's voice was shaky, and even though her great aunt sounded sincere, taking care of her grandmother would take a toll on Jessica. While Catherine appreciated her great aunt's good intentions, she hadn't gotten a realistic dose of how erratic her grandmother's behavior could become.

"What's wrong?" Catherine asked as she put a hand to her chest and focused on her grandmother who had pushed Jessica away.

"This woman is in our *haus*, and I don't understand why." Her grandmother covered her face with her hands and cried.

Catherine gave Jessica a sympathetic look. "Sorry," she said softly.

Her great-aunt didn't acknowledge Catherine's comment, only focused on her sister. "It's okay that you don't know me. I'm a friend of Catherine's and a guest in your house. My name is Jessica."

Catherine's grandmother uncovered her tear-streaked face. "*Mei* apologies. It's very nice to meet you." Her grandma took a handkerchief from the pocket of her black apron and dabbed at her eyes. "I get confused sometimes."

"That's all right." Jessica led her back to the couch, and both women sat. "As a guest in your house, I would like to make you some chicken and dumplings. How does that sound?" She looked at Catherine. "Would that be okay with you?"

Catherine nodded. "*Ya*, that would be lovely. We should have all the ingredients. But as a guest, you shouldn't be—"

"I don't mind," Jessica quickly said without taking her eyes from her sister.

"It's *mei* favorite meal," Catherine's grandmother said, which was news to Catherine. She wasn't sure she'd ever prepared chicken and dumplings for her grandmother.

"I know it is your favorite meal." Jessica smiled. "It's our mother's recipe."

Catherine watched as her grandmother pinched her lips together and squinted her eyebrows, resembling a woman who was trying hard to recall something. Catherine had seen the look many times.

"It's our *mudder's* recipe." Her grandmother smiled, her eyes twinkling as she stared at Jessica with recollection.

"That's right. We have the same mother." Jessica took her grandmother's hand in hers. "And I'm your sister."

Her grandmother's bottom lip trembled as she glanced back and forth between Catherine and Jessica. "I realize that." She bit her bottom lip as if trying to stop the tremble. "I forget things. I get confused." She glanced at Catherine. "And *mei* poor granddaughter has been putting up with me for years."

"I don't mind, *Mammi*," Catherine quickly said.

"I know your granddaughter loves you very much, and she would do anything for you." She glanced at Catherine. "I am here to stay for as long as I'm needed. I want to get to know my sister again."

Catherine forced a smile. "That is nice of you to offer."

And, as much as she appreciated the good intentions of this kind stranger in her house, Catherine suspected it wouldn't last.

CHAPTER 17

a few weeks later . . .
Jessica stayed true to her word, and her help with Catherine's grandmother had been a blessing. Catherine had been shopping on her own, reconnected with friends over lunch, and even gone to an auction to purchase a new milking cow. Even though her aunt had put her house on the market, had certain items shipped to her, and forwarded her mail, Catherine couldn't help but feel that she was on borrowed time. Jessica had already stayed longer than Catherine thought she would.

As she got dressed and readied herself for the day, she glanced at the stack of envelopes on her nightstand. Noah wrote her every other day, and she always wrote him back. It would have been easy for their letters to become mundane and eventually non-existent, but their correspondence only strengthened their bond.

Noah was hoping to come for a visit soon since it was a slower time for their business during the holidays . But it seemed like every time he tried to make plans to come see her, a work emergency or the weather seemed to get in the way.

Her grandmother and great-aunt were in the kitchen having coffee and muffins when there was a knock at the door. Catherine peered out the door and saw a horse and buggy tethered to the fence. It was a clear day, but the temperatures had dipped into single digits.

"Get in here," she said to Ruth, whose teeth were chattering as she stepped into the warm house. Catherine had paid a local boy to split and stack firewood outside the mudroom, and she'd had a fire going continuously for days. "You must be frozen."

Ruth didn't take off her black cape or coat. "I can't stay," she said as she walked to the fireplace, peeled off black gloves, and lowered her palms near the warmth of the fire.

Catherine nodded. "That's fine. I'm happy you stopped by just the same. *Mammi* is having a *gut* day." Her friend had also kept her word and stopped by often to help with Catherine's grandmother.

Ruth spun around, sighed, and shook her head. "*Nee*, Catherine. I mean, I can't stay. I can't stay here in Indiana. I'm returning to Pennsylvania."

Catherine's jaw dropped. As far as she knew, things with Ruth and Leroy had been good. And since Ruth was living at The Peony Inn with two matchmaking elderly sisters, Catherine assumed a marriage announcement would be coming any day. "What? Why?" she finally asked Ruth with a bit more shock than she had intended.

"Leroy is a wonderful, kind man." She raised her chin, as Ruth was known to do, but it didn't stop the tears from pooling in the corners of her eyes. "He's just not the right man for me."

"*Ach*, Ruth." She went to her friend, who had truly become her best friend, and hugged her. "I'm so sorry." She eased away and locked eyes with her. "Are you sure? Did something happen? You seem so happy together."

In truth, Catherine didn't see them together much. Leroy lived in a different district and didn't attend the same church. A visit here, a visit there, but she really hadn't gotten to know Leroy much better than when he'd stayed at her house.

"We were happy." Ruth sniffled, but quickly regained composure, another Ruth attribute. And Catherine caught the past tense in her sentence. "But we don't see eye-to-eye on too many things, and he wants a dozen *kinner*." She rolled her eyes. "I come from a large family, and I don't want more than four *kinner*. I'm not saying that was the deal breaker." She shrugged. "There were other things too." Pausing, she said, "He's too much like *mei daed*. Controlling." She smiled even though her eyes were still moist. "I'm not really the type of woman who can be controlled."

No matter what kind of woman Ruth thought herself to be, she was sad, possibly heartbroken, based on this side of Ruth that Catherine hadn't seen. "When are you leaving?" she asked.

"Later today. I borrowed Lizzie's buggy to come and tell you. And, if she's up for it, I'd like to tell your *mammi* goodbye, and Jessica too." She bowed her head. "I'm sorry I didn't tell you sooner, but goodbyes are hard for me."

Catherine nodded. It would be hard for her to bid farewell to Ruth.

So far, Catherine's grandmother had her wits about her today. The doctor had recently prescribed a new medication that seemed to be helping, allowing her grandmother longer periods of normalcy. There was no guarantee as to how long the medicine would help, but she was grateful for the extended periods when her grandmother was lucid. She hoped these goodbyes wouldn't send her grandmother into a tailspin, which would be difficult for all involved, especially Ruth since she'd grown fond of Catherine's grandmother.

Catherine wanted details. What exactly had gone wrong between Leroy and Ruth? Was it truly just a struggle for control? She would let Ruth share what she was comfortable telling her..

As she recalled the correspondence she'd had back and forth with Noah, and considering this new information, she wondered if spending time together would have led her and Noah to a dead-end path also.

"Follow me." Catherine motioned with her hand. "*Mammi* and Jessica are in kitchen." She said a quick prayer that the conversation would go smoothly for all involved. As easily as possible under the circumstances.

"*Wie bischt*," her grandmother said when Ruth walked in beside Catherine. "It's always lovely to see you." Then her grandmother's smile faded. "What's wrong? You look like you've been crying."

Ruth took a seat beside Catherine's grandmother. "I'm going home, Mary Marie, back to Pennsylvania. But I wanted to personally tell you goodbye. I have enjoyed getting to know you, and I will miss you." She glanced at Jessica, who lowered her head with an unspoken understanding of what was happening.

"Why?" Catherine's grandmother narrowed her eyebrows, frowning. "I thought you and Leroy would end up getting married. Didn't you drink Lizzie and Esther's magic brew?"

Catherine pinched her lips together to avoid smiling.

Ruth sighed. "Mary Marie, you wouldn't believe how much tea, coffee, and lemonade I consumed at The Peony Inn."

"Hmm . . ." Catherine's grandmother frowned. "I'm sad to hear this for you . . . and for me. I will miss you."

"I will miss you, too, but I will write to you all." Ruth stood and smiled at Jessica. "You have certainly been a Godsend, and I will miss you too." She leaned down and gave each woman a hug before she abruptly left the kitchen. Catherine followed.

At the door, Ruth said, "I will miss you most of all." Then she clung to Catherine as if she would never see her again. And she might not.

"Please write." Ruth kissed her on the cheek, then quickly left.

Catherine watched her out the window. Again, she wondered if that would have happened to her and Noah if they had stayed together. Would they have realized that while they were attracted to each other, they didn't share enough in common? It didn't feel like that in their letters, but she wished she would have had an opportunity to find out in person.

After Ruth's buggy turned the corner and was out of

sight, Catherine placed another log on the fire before she joined her grandmother and her great-aunt.

"*Ach*, that was a surprise," her grandmother said before she took a sip of coffee. Catherine silently thanked God that the conversation had gone smoothly.

Catherine pulled out a chair beside her grandmother and sat, sighing. "*Ya*, I will really miss her."

Jessica cleared her throat. "Catherine, we want to talk to you about something."

"It's not anything bad," her grandmother added.

Catherine picked at a splinter she'd gotten earlier on a piece of firewood. "What's that?"

"We want you to go to Pennsylvania and spend time with Noah," her grandmother said.

Catherine looked up, her eyebrows raised as she lowered her hand. "What?" Her grandmother and great-aunt hadn't had time to process the fact that Ruth was leaving, so this must have been something on their minds already.

Her grandmother reached into her pocket and pulled out one of Noah's letters. Catherine felt her blood boil. "How—"

"You left it in the guest bathroom on the counter." Her grandmother slid the envelope across the table. "I'm sorry, but I read it. And Jessica and I both think you need to visit that man. Those feelings need to be investigated."

A blush climbed up Catherine's neck, and a burning embarrassment filled her cheeks. "Those are private letters, *Mammi*."

"*Ya*, but it was there, and I read it." Her grandmother shrugged. "And you need to go visit him."

162

Catherine had been safely writing her feelings about most things to Noah. Seeing him in person would feel different, exposed. Even though it sparked excitement at the thought of spending time with him, she hadn't thought about it as a possibility—because it wasn't doable.

"I have *mei* sister here to take care of me, *mei* sweet *maed*. It's time you live your life." Her grandmother spoke firmly.

"I want to stay here, Catherine," Jessica said. "Over the past few weeks, I've gotten to know you and my sister. Please let me do this for you." She paused. "And for me and Mary Marie. I know we talk about things that don't interest you. We have so many childhood memories that we recall. The good and the bad, but they're ours to share, and we need that."

Catherine wanted to ask Jessica how it felt to relive the exact conversation repeatedly as if they hadn't just discussed a certain subject the day before. While the medication helped her grandmother, it certainly hadn't eliminated her symptoms.

"*Nee*. I can't." Her grandmother was everything to Catherine, the mother she hadn't really had. She wasn't going to leave her. "You saw what happened with Ruth and Leroy. It didn't work out."

"That doesn't mean it won't work out for you and Noah. And it sounds like . . ." Jessica chewed her bottom lip. "Sorry, I read the letter too. It sounds like Noah's job makes it harder for him to come here. You have me now. Take advantage of this opportunity and go spend time with that young man."

"I can't leave—"

"*Ya*, you can," her grandmother said firmly. She pulled her hand into hers. "Catherine, *mei lieb*, I know what is happening to me. *Mei* mind is going to deteriorate to a point where I don't know you at all. I won't know Jessica. And I might not even know *mei* own name." She paused, blinking back tears. "Make me happy and go find your future. I am the only thing keeping you from doing so, and I won't have that."

She glared at Jessica. "Did you talk her into this?"

Jessica's eyes widened. "I don't think so. We discussed it and both agree that you should have a life of your own."

"I have a life." Catherine had lost any excitement about the prospect of seeing Noah, be it him coming here or her going there. She felt pushed out of her own life. "I have been taking care of *mei mammi* for four years."

"And you have done a wonderful job." Jessica reached her hand across the table toward Catherine's, but Catherine moved hers away.

She thought about all the times it had taken them both to calm down her grandmother, one of them always on call to watch her, and what if she had one of her bad episodes, like throwing a perfectly good food across the rom because she said it tasted bad? Or threatening to bite one of them if she didn't get her way about something? Those type of episodes didn't happen often, but when they did, it was horrific.

"*Nee*, I'm not leaving." She roughly pushed back her chair, the legs grinding against the wood floor as she stood. *I will not be evicted from the only home I've ever known. Not even for a man.* Her grandmother needed her. Jessica had only been here a short time, "And it's not up for discussion again."

IT WAS LATER in the evening, after her grandmother and aunt were in their beds, when Catherine carried her lantern and tiptoed into the kitchen. She startled when she saw Jessica sitting in the dark.

"What are you doing just sitting here?" Catherine held the lantern up to see the woman who resembled her mother, close in age and appearance. That seemed to be all the two women had in common.

"I couldn't sleep," Jessica said with a glass of milk in front of her, dressed in a dark blue robe, her grayish hair swept into a twist on her head. She didn't have on any makeup—something she'd given up shortly after her arrival. While she hadn't completely embraced the Amish way of life, she seemed to slowly be working her way back to a life she once knew. She gathered eggs, had taken to wearing some of Catherine's grandmother's dresses, and she cooked and baked a lot. Her short hair, which had grown since her arrival, was a reminder that that she wasn't Amish, but overall, she seemed to be relaxing into their ways.

Catherine placed the lantern in the middle of the table, poured herself a glass of milk, and sat across from Jessica. "I'm sorry if I sounded harsh earlier." She took a sip from her glass. "But I have been taking care of *mei mammi* for a long time. I don't think you understand how hard it can be sometimes."

"I understand more than you think." She slumped into her chair as she circled the rim of her glass with one finger. "My husband suffered from dementia for the last two years of his life. I know how hard it is."

Guilt flooded over Catherine when she realized that she hadn't asked much about her aunt's life. "I'm sorry," she said. "I really am. But you know that everything we spoke about tonight, *Mammi* might not remember in the morning. And what if she starts calling you Catherine? She called me Jessica for years. I didn't even think you were real."

"Then I'll be Catherine that day," she said with a small smile. "There's something you don't understand."

Catherine thought she saw things quite clearly, but she waited.

"When Mary Marie tells me the same story repeatedly, I learn something new each time. Some of the experiences we had, only the two of us share. Our childhood. The good and the bad. Mary Marie is so much older than me that she knows things I don't. I enjoy hearing her stories—most of them." She paused, seemingly back in her childhood for a few moments. "But our conversations, no matter how many times they are repeated, is healing for us in many ways. We are getting a second chance to know each other even if it's for brief intervals." She smiled. "One time, my husband went six weeks without one episode. I cherished that time. Oh, there were difficult stretches for sure, but the good times have a way of making up for it."

Catherine could read between the lines. "You are trying to say that *mei* leaving would be a *gut* thing for you and *Mammi* so that I wouldn't feel guilty about going to see Noah."

Jessica shrugged. "Partly. Because I don't want you to feel guilty. But I'm not lying about the rest of it. There is a bond between sisters that is solid no matter how much time passes or what our mental faculties might be. We are the keepers of each other's childhood, memories that no one shares but us. Your grandmother remembers things I don't, and sometimes we recall things very differently. But together, these are our memories, and ours alone." She was quiet for a while. "Please just think about it. What if Noah is the one that got away because you never had an opportunity to spend time with him?"

Catherine stayed quiet. The thought of seeing Noah finally caused her heart to flutter.

"He has never invited me to come visit him," she finally said, a reality that stung a little.

"What would you have told him?" Jessica tipped her head to one side.

"*Nee.* I would have told him *nee.*"

"And he knows that. Give him a chance to be open to the idea of you visiting him." Jessica finished the rest of her milk. "I feel like I can sleep now."

After saying goodnight, Jessica left Catherine alone with her thoughts in the kitchen, her lantern almost out of oil, barely flickering in the darkness. Then it went out. And she sat in the darkness for the next hour, not feeling like she could sleep at all. What if this was her chance to find happiness? Or would something awful happen to her grandmother while she was away? It felt too heavy on her heart to consider.

CHAPTER 18

*N*oah could barely believe his eyes the day he'd opened the door of his farmhouse. There she'd stood. Catherine. He'd known she was coming for a visit, but doubts had plagued him even though they'd made extensive plans for her to come and stay for a week at a nearby Amish bed and breakfast. The bishop had granted her permission to fly, seeming to understand that her situation warranted an exception to the rules.

She'd been early that day. He hadn't shaved yet. He recalled his feelings and the conversation.

"Wie bischt," she'd said softly as she blushed. "I'm early."

There had been so many letters and occasional phone calls. But when she was standing in front of him, he was frozen in place, his feet rooted to the wooden porch steps beneath his feet. "That's okay," he told her before pulling her into a hug. "I can't believe you're actually here." He eased her to arm's length as he kept his hands on her upper arms, his eyes locking with hers. Then he pulled

169

her close again before he threw caution to the wind, tenderly held her cheeks, and kissed her the way he had at Thanksgiving. And it had been as if no time had passed.

Noah had introduced her to his family that evening, and for the next week, he'd worked less hours—with his father's approval—and spent his time away from work showing her around Lancaster County. Every evening, they watched the sunset on his porch, kissed passionately, and rode in his buggy to the bed and breakfast where she was staying. While he was at work, she spent time with Ruth, his mother, and his other sisters. She felt like family.

But after a week of this routine, she was set to go home the following morning.

"Don't go," he said as they kissed goodnight outside of the bed and breakfast where she'd been staying. "Now, that you're here, I want you to stay forever." He knew what he was asking her, and he had no qualms about his words, which echoed his heart.

"I want to, but I can't," she said. "*Mei mammi . . .*"

"I know." He drew her closer, his hand cupping the back of her head, his fingers brushing against the loose strands of hair that had escaped her prayer covering. Saying goodbye this time was far worse than before, as if a part of himself was leaving, and he wasn't sure he would ever feel whole again. Still holding her, he said, "What are we going to do?"

Her face was molded against his blue shirt, and he could feel the moisture from her eyes. "I don't know."

Noah knew what he had to do. "I'll quit *mei* job working for *mei* father and move to Indiana."

She began to shake her head. "*Nee, nee.* Your father

depends on you." She eased away and put a soft hand on his face. "I want to be with you, always, but our situations don't allow it."

"There must be a way. And I will figure it out." Noah had been pondering how to keep her here since the first day she arrived. Why hadn't he come up with a solution before now? Then it hit him like a bolt of lightning that didn't kill him but electrocuted him into action. He dropped to one knee. "Will you marry me, Catherine?"

Her jaw dropped.

"Just marry me, and we can figure out everything else." He held both her hands in his while she stood staring down at him with wide eyes. "I *lieb* you."

"Noah, I *lieb* you too, but . . ." Her voice cracked as she spoke. "I can't stay. You know that. *Mei* parents didn't do right by *mei mammi*, and even though Aunt Jessica is there, I feel a responsibility to return to her."

He slowly stood, still holding both her hands. "I know how much you *lieb* her." He couldn't fault her for that, but there had to be some way for them to be together. "I'll figure something out." He had no idea what. Why was God punishing them this way? His father's business put food on the table for his entire family. And it didn't work without Noah. And Catherine had a loyalty to her grandmother, another quality he admired about her even if it prevented them from being together.

"After I check *mei* flight time this evening, I'll make arrangements for a driver. I just need to let the owner of the B&B know what time I travel.," she said through tears.

"I don't know how to say goodbye to you again." His

heart felt like it would explode as he kissed her one final time.

"I *lieb* you," she said before swiping at her eyes, then she closed the door.

~

FOLLOWING A SLEEPLESS NIGHT, Catherine was up at five o'clock in the morning. She dressed, packed up her toiletries, and prepared for her trip home. Her aunt had told her on the phone that it was an afternoon flight. Flying from Indiana to Pennsylvania had been her first time to fly. She'd been exhilarated by the adventure and her eagerness to see Noah. Now, she felt anxious about the flight, sadder than ever before, and cheated out of an opportunity for love. A long-distance relationship wasn't logical or feasible. And, just to fly in an airplane required approval from the bishop. It was usually reserved for funerals, but luckily their current bishop wasn't as conservative as the older bishop before him. He still wouldn't allow her to make a practice of flying. It was also no way to have a relationship.

She sat on the bed of the quaint bed and breakfast room she'd called home for her time in Lancaster County. It was small, but lovely, and less than a mile from Noah's farmhouse, located on family property. Ruth also had her own farmhouse on the property. Ruth had reiterated to Catherine that Leroy was a wonderful man, but that after spending time with him, she didn't feel the way she should about someone in a romantic relationship. Catherine felt everything a person should feel, and yet she would be walking away from it. From Noah.

Please, Gott, *please. How can Noah and I be together without hurting our families?*

Every time Catherine had spoken to her great aunt—whom she'd accepted as such and come to love—Jessica insisted that everything was fine, while also admitting to the progression of her grandmother's illness. The new medication wasn't working as well as in the beginning. If Catherine didn't go home soon, her grandmother might not know her at all, ever, and that was too much to bear.

She found the sealed envelope marked "Return Flight" in the inner side pocket of her suitcase, written in her grandmother's handwriting. She'd kept it out of sight during her trip. She didn't need another reminder that her situation was temporary. She peeled back the seal, then opened the white paper inside. But it wasn't a return ticket. It was a letter from her grandmother.

Dear Catherine,

I'm sure you are surprised to find this letter instead of a return ticket home. This was never a roundtrip adventure, only a one-way ticket toward happiness. I cannot speak to your parents' decisions because we aren't on this earth to judge. Only Gott *can do that. What I can say is that you have selflessly cared for me over the past four years while giving up the life you should be living. Please let me give something back to you—your freedom.*

Jessica has committed to mei *long-term care, and during the times when I am mentally stable, we enjoy reliving our child-hood. We lost way too many years. Of course, I have bad days when I can't recall why your great aunt is here, and sometimes I* can't remember her name or the fact that she is *mei* only sibling.

Please don't come home. This will be the greatest gift you can give me. By the time you read this, I might have already slipped into a place where I've forgotten you completely. How painful that would be for you to see me that way. And somewhere deep inside of *mei* lost memories, I believe I would still feel a level of hurt even if I can't remember your name or know the love that you have shown me.

Was it presumptuous of me to assume that you and Noah would fall in *lieb* during your time there? *Nee.* I saw the way you looked at each other and interacted together. Ruth and Leroy were temporarily smitten, but it did not surprise me when Ruth chose to go back to Pennsylvania. I didn't see in her eyes what I saw between you and Noah. Ruth visited often while she was here, and she would make a wonderful sister-in-law for you. She is wise and kind.

So, in closing *mei* beautiful *maed,* allow yourself to be happy. During your phone calls—the ones I remember—you sounded like the young woman I always wanted you to become . . . someone in *lieb.*

Latch on to this opportunity. Again, by the time you get home, *mei lieb,* I might not know you at all. It's the harsh reality of *mei* condition.

Stay in Pennsylvania. *Gott* whispered in *mei* ear that's where you should be. You don't want to go against *Gott,* do you?

Sending you all *mei lieb* and blessings,

Grandmammi

P.S. – Jessica helped me write parts of this letter, but the feelings are all mine.

Tears streamed down Catherine's cheeks as she re-read the letter two more times, then she called her grandmother's mobile phone, praying that it would be turned on, that she would answer, and that she would be herself. But it was Jessica who answered. Catherine was almost too choked up to speak, but she managed to say, "I'm coming home."

CHAPTER 19

*S*till sitting on her bed and crying, Catherine listened to her great aunt, knowing she would not be able to change her mind. *I'm going home.*

"Your grandmother meant every word of that letter, Catherine. She wants you to stay there and make a life for yourself. She was insistent on writing to you when she was feeling her best and with her mental state intact. I only had to help her a little."

"I can't, Aunt Jessica," Catherine said through tears. "I need to be there with her."

"Catherine . . ." There was a long pause. "Since she wrote that letter, she has had more bad days than good. It is important to her that you remember her how she was. She loves you so very much. The only acceptable reason for you to come home is if things did not work out with you and Noah, and I very much doubt that is the case. This is basically her dying wish, for you to be happy. Are you happy with Noah?"

Catherine recalled Noah proposing to her. At the time, it felt too out of reach to consider it as a true proposal. "*Ya*, but it doesn't matter because—"

"It *does* matter. It's what your grandmother wants. I can take care of her, but I also arranged for home health care to visit. I am aware her situation will continue to decline. But I missed so much time with my sister, and it gives me so much joy to take care of her, to be there for those good days and bad days. Now, tell me . . . are you in love with Noah?"

Catherine sniffled. "*Ya*, very much so. But I can't imagine not seeing *Mammi* again."

"Then see her in your mind's eye, the vivacious, healthy woman whom you love. Because if she continues to decline the way the doctor said at her last appointment, she will eventually not know any of us, and I fear that time is coming soon."

"And that's why I need to come home now, where there is still the possibility that she will know me." Catherine couldn't image not seeing her grandmother, even if she didn't know her.

"Sweet child." Jessica sighed. "I can't tell you what to do. Right now, your grandmother is napping. She didn't know who I was this morning, and that's okay. I know who she is. Catherine, you took care of her for so long. There is no shame in choosing the life she wants for you. To not do so, is going against her wishes. But you must decide for yourself."

Catherine sat with a hand to her forehead as a headache from too much crying persisted. "I-I need to think about this."

"Okay," Jessica said sympathetically. "But I know that you will honor your grandmother's final wishes."

After they hung up, Catherine stood, went to the sink in the bathroom, and splashed water on her face. Afterward, she removed her prayer covering and let her brown locks spill past her waist, then stared at herself in the mirror. No man had ever seen her hair out from beneath her prayer covering. She closed her eyes and envisioned Noah running his hands the length of her hair, the way he cupped her cheeks with strong hands when he kissed her. And her mind traveled back to her grandmother making snow angels and the kindness Noah had shown them both.

She thought about the past week, the happiest week of her life. Did God really tell her grandmother that she should stay?

Catherine read the letter again.

NOAH PUT the final stain on a dining room table out in his father's shop where they worked. There hadn't been much conversation between the two men. Noah was afraid to speak for fear he might burst into tears and lose all sense of dignity in his father's presence.

But after a while, his father cleared his throat. "You miss the *maed*, Catherine?" he said as he wiped his hands on a towel he kept over his shoulder.

Noah didn't look up, just nodded. Then he silently prayed that God would put the notion in his father's head to let him out of this family commitment, to encourage him to go to Indiana to be with Catherine, who was probably already at the airport by now, a thought that shredded his insides.

His father began sanding a chair that matched the table Noah was working on. "She seems like a nice *maed*, and you certainly seem smitten with her."

"*Ya.*" Noah waited to see if moving to Indiana was an option for him, but another ten minutes of silence ensued.

"I'll tell you what . . ." His father straightened from where he had been squatting in the shop. He wiped his hands on the towel again. "If this is true *lieb*, it seems a shame for me to stand in the way of your happiness."

Noah's ears perked up, afraid to get his hopes up too much. He'd been repeatedly told how their family company couldn't function without him.

"If it is true *lieb*," his dad went on, "then it should stand the test of time. Give me three months to find a suitable replacement for you. You should be able to set up your own construction company in Indiana."

Noah wasn't sure he was hearing him correctly. "In three months, I can leave?"

His father shrugged. "You're a twenty-seven-year-old man. You should be able to choose your destiny, and if it's with Catherine, then your *mamm* and I don't want to stand in the way of that."

Noah couldn't believe what he was hearing. "*Daed* . . ." He swallowed back a knot in his throat. Even though his dream was becoming a reality, there was still a level of sadness that he would be away from his family. But he wanted Catherine as his wife. He was sure of it. "*Danki.* I'll make sure we find someone who will be skilled enough to help you keep things running without a hitch."

His father chuckled. "And when you have *kinner* with that woman, ask *Gott* to give you more than one *sohn* to help in the fields and family businesses."

Noah smiled. *"Danki, Daed,"* he said again before putting a hand to his forehead. "I've got to let her know."

He rushed out of the barn just as a plane flew high in the sky above him. Was she in the air, waiting on her flight, or already home?

Noah rushed to his buggy where he kept his cell phone. He was dialing her number when a car came up the driveway. Holding the phone, he waited to see what English person had come to visit. They didn't have many English visitors.

He dropped the phone as his feet took on a mind of their own and began hurrying toward the car. "Catherine," he said, breathless, when he reached her. "I thought you would be gone by now."

She smiled as she handed him a folded-up letter. He read it with a heavy heart, but also with an anxious undertone of emotions. "Does this mean . . ." He was nervous to ask. ". . . that you're staying?"

After she nodded, he pulled her into his arms. "I *lieb* you so much. I was beginning to wonder if I would ever be happy without you in *mei* life." He eased her away. "But are you sure about this?"

She nodded. "I am. Before she became sick, *mei mammi* was a strong woman with conviction, and knowing I might not ever see her again is difficult." She paused. "But

I'd rather she knows that I'm happy, which is what she truly wants. I just wish that I could see her one more time."

Noah kissed her the way he'd been imagining all day. "I am going to pray every day for the next three months that your *mammi's* mind will grow stronger and that she'll know you."

"Three months?" Catherine gazed at him, her eyes twinkling but misty.

"That's how long I have to find *mei* replacement. *Daed* has given us his blessing to be together in Indiana."

"Really?" She bounced up on her toes and smiled, but she sobered quickly. "But what about your family? They'll miss you terribly." The only family Catherine had in Indiana was her grandmother and her great-aunt. She no longer counted her parents as family, although she prayed for them daily. She'd reconnected with friends since her aunt's arrival, and Lizzie and Esther still visited regularly, although they still questioned their matchmaking skills related to Leroy and Ruth. Catherine thought about her relationships at home and was still pondering how to tell Noah her plan when he spoke.

"And I'll miss them. But *mei* sisters will find husbands and start families of their own, and we will visit them as often as we can. I want you to be *mei* family, Catherine." He dropped to one knee again. "Will you marry me? I promise to *lieb* you for the rest of *mei* life."

CATHERINE GAZED upon the man who had stolen her heart at Thanksgiving when they met. She reflected on her grandmother's letter. And she nodded. "*Ya*, Noah, I will marry you." Her heart pounded in her chest at the idea of being Noah's wife.

Amish weddings usually took place in the fall, in October or November, after the harvest. As much as she wanted to marry Noah, and she would, she wished that her grandmother could see her get married, solidifying what she wanted for her—true love and happiness. But her grandmother was frail, and she wouldn't be able to make such a long trip here to Pennsylvania even with her great aunt helping her. But Catherine would keep true to her grandmother's wishes and stay with Noah, make a life with him, and have his children. She briefly thought about her parents and what they would miss out on in the future, but they had made their own life choices. And now, Catherine had to believe that it was her time for joy. But she wasn't going to make Noah give up his large family and roots that ran for generations to pursue a life with her."I want us to live here," she said. "I want to grow into your life here, to know your family better, for our *kinner* to know their cousins and aunts and uncles. I want them to fish in the creek where you fished when you were a boy. I missed out on a big family."

"Are you sure?" Noah's eyes watered. "What about your *grandmammi*?"

Catherine closed her eyes and pictured her grandmother in her mind's eye. Then she looked into the eyes of the man she would marry. "This is what she wants for me."

"I *lieb* you, Catherine."

"And I *lieb* you." She closed her eyes and leaned into his kiss, filled with love . . . and excitement about her future and all that God had planned for her and Noah.

Please take care of Mammi, Gott.

Catherine kissed her husband-to-be again, giving all the thanks and praise to God.

EPILOGUE

Catherine and Noah stood outside the home she'd grown up in as their driver carried their bags up the driveway. They'd traveled mostly by bus for this trip, which had been exhausting, but also exhilarating. It had been a year since she'd met Noah during the Thanksgiving storm. Only now, Noah was her husband. She wished her great aunt and grandmother could have been at her wedding, but her grandmother's condition hadn't allowed it. They'd been married in the spring even though the timing was untraditional.

Noah had a strong arm looped with hers as they slowly made their way toward the house. The weather was a far cry from what it was a year ago. The sun shone brightly without a cloud in the sky, and the wind breezed through her as was typical for the beginning of the holiday season.

Then she stopped abruptly.

"I'm scared," she said as she stopped ten feet from the porch steps.

"I know."

Catherine had kept in contact with her grandmother and aunt since she'd chosen to stay in Pennsylvania. Her grandmother had more bad days than good, and Catherine was always happy when their phone calls went well. She was elated to receive letters from her in the mail, although her beautiful cursive writing had become harder and harder to read.

"What if this is a bad day and she doesn't know me?" Catherine's chest ached at the thought.

"You will know her, and she will feel your *lieb.*" Noah took a slow step, encouraging Catherine to put one foot in front of the other until they were standing at the door of the home she'd spent most of her life in. She could smell the aroma of turkey cooking on the other side of the front door. It felt odd to knock at what used to be her home, and she shook from head to toe, mostly from nerves and not the cool breeze.

The wood door opened slowly, and her grandmother smiled through the screen. Would she think Catherine was a salesperson? Would she send her away? How distraught would she become if she didn't recognize the person who stood in front of her?

Catherine knew how upset she would be if her grandmother didn't recognize her, but she would smile and make it through Thanksgiving Day, keeping in mind what her husband had said. *She will feel your* lieb. She held her breath but released it when her grandmother held out her arms. Catherine ran to her filled with faith, hope, and love.

"*Wie bischt, mei* sweet granddaughter, Catherine. You make *mei* heart smile."

Catherine was sure her own heart smiled even brighter as she held onto her grandmother, grateful for this Thanksgiving Day and all her future had in store for her.

A REQUEST

Authors depend on reviews from readers. If you enjoyed this book, would you please consider leaving a review on AMAZON.

READING GROUP GUIDE FOR AN AMISH THANKSGIVING

1. Catherine does a good job of keeping her cool because she realizes that her grandmother can't help what is happening to her. But she is human and can't always control her emotions. What are some examples of her showing her true feelings?

2. Esther and Lizzie, previously featured in the *Amish Inn* series and *An Amish Matchmaker* are up to their old tricks again. How many times do they play matchmaker in this story?

3. Have you ever cared for a loved one who suffered from dementia or Alzheimer's? If so, could you relate to Catherine?

4. Noah has a tender heart. What are some examples of his kind gestures, with Catherine and others in the story?

5. Were you surprised that Ruth and Leroy didn't end up together? Or did you think they were a sure thing? Explain.

6. Catherine's parents, Sarah and Amos, left their Amish district, got a divorce, and are uninvolved in Catherine's life. Her mother barely acknowledges Catherine's willingness to give up her future to care for her grandmother. How did this make you feel? Should Catherine have been more forceful with her mother, firmly suggesting she come home and help with her grandmother? Or was it a selfless act of love and shouldn't have been judged or questioned?

7. Family is sometimes the people we choose. Does God put certain people in our lives in an effort to form a family unit that isn't the one we were born into? How did you see this happening with the characters in this story?

8. If you could change anything about the book, what would it be? Would you have Ruth and Leroy live happily ever after, or does that not equate with reality, that everything can't end up perfectly for everyone?

9. If you could choose to be any character in the story—and modify their actions/reactions—who would you choose to be and why? What would you do differently?

TURN THE PAGE TO READ A
SAMPLE OF AN AMISH
CHRISTMAS GIFT

INCLUDES
AMISH RECIPES

AN
AMISH
CHRISTMAS GIFT
A SHORT STORY

BETH
WISEMAN
BESTSELLING AUTHOR

AN AMISH CHRISTMAS GIFT - CHAPTER 1

*H*annah King wished she could skip Christmas this year even though she'd always treasured the holiday and everything it represented. She forced herself to wrap gifts while her children spent time at their aunt and uncle's house on this crisp December morning. The aroma of freshly baked bread hung in the air, orange embers crackled as they shimmied up the fireplace, and she'd organized the children's presents from where she sat on her living room floor—just like she'd done every year. She was surrounded by various rolls of wrapping paper, colorful bows she'd made from ribbon purchased at the market, and an assortment of boxes.

As was tradition, they wouldn't have a Christmas tree, but Hannah would place the wrapped gifts around the living room to create a festive atmosphere. She'd already laid out garland atop the fireplace mantel and placed poinsettias on either side of the stone structure while her two daughters helped decorate other areas. Lillian, who had just turned seven, had attached red bows on the porch columns outside and created a lovely centerpiece for the dining room table using pinecones, red and green ribbons, and holly. Eighteen-year-old Mae had unpacked other decorations they kept stored in the basement and placed them around the house. Hannah hoped that being with her sister's family for the day might infuse some holiday joy into her daughters' lives.

Ruth and Henry didn't have children of their own yet, and they doted on Hannah's girls. Spoiled them was more like it. And that was okay with Hannah. It was their first Christmas without Paul, her beloved husband and father of the two beautiful girls. A life taken much too early.

Hannah slipped the pink sweater she'd knitted for Lillian into a box. Her youngest daughter could still get away with wearing pastel colors at her age, and pink was Lillian's favorite color. She chose red and white striped wrapping paper, but she hadn't even closed the box when she covered her face with both hands and cried, the type of sobbing that people do only when they are alone. Her grief shook her to the core and often came on unexpectedly. Hannah did her best to stay strong for Lillian and Mae and never showed her emotions around them. She hadn't cried in front of anyone since the funeral, not even her sister, to whom she'd always been close. It was her job, as a mother, to be strong for her girls, and feigning strength around everyone else was good practice, albeit difficult.

Today, she needed the release, and shipping the girls to Ruth and Henry was about more than just needing privacy to wrap presents. She needed the solitude to let go of some of the grief that had such a firm hold on her, a type of suffocation that left her feeling as though she couldn't breathe sometimes. Hopefully, she could get it out of her system before the girls returned. It had been six months since the accident that took her husband's life at only forty-one years old. She couldn't help but wonder if she would always feel the stabbing pain in her chest that represented the void in her life.

MAE ENJOYED BEING with her Aunt Ruth and Uncle Henry. Even though they had loved her father, she supposed it was easier for them to get on with life than it was for Mae, her sister, and her mother. There was a giant hole in their hearts, and even with all the Christmas decorations at home, the absence of their father, the void, the changes, the sadness . . . it hovered in the air like a dark cloud that would never produce rain or go away. The worst part was hearing her mother crying herself to sleep every night, only to pretend everything was okay when she was around Mae and her sister. Lillian was only seven and didn't have as many memories to hold onto as Mae. But after twenty years of marriage, it was her mother who seemed to be suffering the most, and it scared Mae.

Amish funerals were a sober affair but showing grief in public was discouraged. As was tradition, Mae's father had been buried three days after his death. Preceding the burial, a viewing was held at their home, followed by a church service, and then her father was laid to rest in the Amish cemetery, his headstone identical to all the others.

Mae's mother had remained stoic and hadn't cried throughout any of the services even though Lillian and Mae shed tears, along with several others. Maybe her mother should have let go of some of her emotions. Was all that grief bottled up inside and spilling out privately at night? How long would her mother suffer? *Forever?*

Mae stood at the window and watched her uncle push Lillian on the swing when her aunt came up beside her.

"How's your *mamm?*" Aunt Ruth was three years younger than her mother, a beautiful woman with auburn hair and green eyes. She told everyone she must be adopted because there wasn't a redhead anywhere in the family tree. Mae's grandparents laughed at the notion and assured everyone Ruth wasn't adopted.

"She's okay." Mae hadn't told anyone that she often heard her mother softly crying late at night. With each new day, she prayed that her mom wouldn't suffer so much. Even though she fought hard to hide it, Mae could see the sadness in her mother's eyes, her daily interactions, and especially during worship service. Maybe the Spirit moved her. Perhaps she begged God to bring back her husband and Lillian and Mae's father.

Her Aunt Ruth put a hand on her back, rubbing gently. "I know it doesn't feel like it right now, but time will ease the pain, and eventually you will all be happy again." She paused, sighing. "Your *daed* was a *gut* man."

Mae's bottom lip trembled. She wasn't as good as her mother when it came to hiding her emotions.

"Look at those two." Aunt Ruth lowered her arm from Mae's back and pointed out the window. "He's going to make a wonderful *daed* someday."

Coming here was an escape from the sadness at her house, and her aunt must have sensed that Mae didn't want to talk about the loss they'd suffered.

Her aunt and uncle had been trying to have a baby for over ten years. There was no medical reason they shouldn't be able to, according to the doctor. Mae had heard about fertility drugs and in vitro fertilization, but most of their people—her aunt and uncle included—believed conception was in God's hands. "And you'll be a wonderful *mudder*," Mae said as she turned to her and smiled.

"We will see." Aunt Ruth spoke with an air of hope marred by a dose of doubt as she grabbed Mae's hand and led her toward the kitchen. "Since we have some time to ourselves, I want to hear about this new boyfriend you have. I mean, I've known the Byler's for years, but it seems like Johnny turned into a man overnight." She pulled out a kitchen chair and motioned for Mae to sit. "I'll pour us some *kaffi*, and I made banana bread this morning."

"He goes by John now, not Johnny." Mae reached for a slice of warm bread after her aunt set two plates and a platter on the table, then she returned with two cups of coffee.

"Your *mamm* said you two are spending a lot of time together." She smiled. "Do you think *John* is the one?"

Mae had gone out with two other boys after she'd turned sixteen and her parents allowed her to date. Each relationship had only lasted a few months and never progressed past a kiss on the cheek. John was different, and deep inside, Mae knew he was the one for her. She'd known him all her life, but his family lived outside of

Montgomery. The town in southern Indiana was small, but John, his parents, and siblings were still part of the same district as Mae and her family. But due to the distance between their homes, she hadn't really gotten to know him until he began working at the lumberyard near her house. They had been seeing each other for three months, ever since she'd gone to the lumberyard to pick up supplies for small repairs needed on their house. She and John had slipped into an easy conversation, and before she left, he had asked her out for supper.

"I don't know if he is the one." Mae swallowed hard. She disliked lying to anyone, especially someone she loved as much as Aunt Ruth. But telling her aunt the truth would cause more heartache for everyone. Mae had already let things get out of hand with John. "We haven't been seeing each other all that long."

Her aunt got a faraway look in her eyes, then smiled as she refocused on Mae. "I knew I *liebed* Henry and that he was the one for me by our third date."

Mae longed to tell her aunt that she'd fallen for John right away, too, but she only forced a smile. "I guess we will see how it goes."

Her aunt took a bite of bread, then dabbed her mouth with her napkin. "When do you see him again?"

"Tonight. He's coming over." Mae's heart fluttered at the thought. Her mother would put Lillian to bed early, then disappear into her bedroom so Mae and John could sit on the couch in the living room and have some time alone. She appreciated her mother's efforts.

"It's supposed to snow." Aunt Ruth lifted her shoulders, grinning, as she clutched her coffee cup between her hands. "So romantic. A warm fire, maybe some hot cider, and your *mamm* will have the house decorated for Christmas. It sounds wonderful."

Mae envisioned the evening, and it would be exactly as her aunt described. She hoped she wouldn't hear her mother crying in her bedroom. She prayed that thoughts of her father wouldn't overtake her emotions and cloud the evening. Grief had stages. She'd read a book about it that Aunt Ruth had given her. Mae knew time would heal her, but she wasn't sure that was the case for her mother, who seemed stuck in a bad place, unable to get past the intense pain, evidenced by her unwillingness to even mention Mae's father and crying herself to sleep almost every night. She did her best to put on a good act during daylight hours by attempting to be cheerful, and Mae was pretty sure her younger sister bought into it, but Mae didn't. For a while, she had thought her mother was getting better. Or her mother had just been better at hiding her emotions during those interludes. Perhaps the holidays had caused her grief to resurface even more.

She forced the thoughts away and cleared her throat. "John is a wonderful man," she finally said in response to her aunt's comments. But she would lose him to another woman eventually because Mae had no plans to marry John Byler.

AN AMISH CHRISTMAS GIFT - CHAPTER 2

*J*ohn cranked up the battery-operated heater in his buggy, pulled his black coat snug around him before he took hold of the reins and backed up, anxious to arrive at Mae's house. She'd have a warm fire going, coffee or hot cider ready, and she'd already told him they had been decorating for Christmas. He wouldn't care if they met in a rundown barn in the woods if he was near her. Being in her arms was all the warmth he needed. But the ambiance she'd described would be the perfect setting for tonight since John had a special surprise for Mae.

Snow swirled in powdery circles like magic fairy dust leading him to his future wife. It was much too soon to propose, but he knew beyond a shadow of a doubt that Mae was the woman he wanted to marry then raise a family. Six children. Three boys and three girls. He smiled to himself as he pictured Mae and their children seated around a big table in the house John would build for them. He'd already purchased a two-acre tract for when the time came to build a home. He'd been saving his money since he'd started working at sixteen, for only two years, but it had been enough to put a down payment on the property.

He spent the rest of his journey daydreaming about the life he and Mae would have. Hopefully, next fall, after the harvest, they would get married.

Everything was blanketed in white by the time he arrived at Mae's house almost forty-five minutes later. He was used to the long buggy ride to work daily. It would have been easier to go straight from work to Mae's house, but he had chores to do at home before he could visit her in the evenings, which made for a lot of traveling. But he'd travel however far he had to so that he could spend time with her.

After he pulled on his black knit cap, he stepped out of the buggy and unhitched his horse, then led the stallion to the lean-to nearby. Mae had already put out fresh oats and water for the animal.

Dodging the snowfall put a spring in John's step as he jogged toward the house with his chin tucked and gloved hands cupped above his eyebrows. His breath clouded in front of him, but it was impossible not to notice the evening light reflecting off the flakes that created a vibrant landscape.

He was stepping out of his boots on the covered front porch when Mae opened the door, smiling.

John was sure his future bride grew more beautiful with each passing day. Her light brown hair was tucked beneath her prayer covering. She'd told him it had grown past her waist, although he wouldn't see the long tresses until they were married. Maybe before, if they went swimming over the summer, or if she allowed him to see her hair down. Some Amish women, his mother being one of them, didn't reveal their hair until marriage. Others were more liberal about the tradition. John wasn't sure what Mae's feelings were on the subject.

"Hurry and get out of your coat. You must be freezing." She bounced up on her toes as she hugged herself to stay warm from the cold air he was letting in.

He slid out of his coat and shook it before draping it over his arm, then popped off his hat and gloves, shaking off as much snow as he could before crossing the threshold to hang the items on the rack inside.

Mae closed the door behind him, then gave him a quick hug. He glanced around the living room filled with holiday decorations as the smell of cinnamon filled his nostrils. They made their way to the fireplace, where he warmed his hands, anxious to cup her cheeks and gaze into her brown eyes before kissing her the way he had been for the past two months. Their first month together had consisted of hugs and kisses on the cheek, but things had evolved into more than a close friendship. They had shared their first passionate kiss behind the barn after worship service at the Lantz's house. He had longed to be in her arms from that moment on. She stayed in his heart and on his mind even when he wasn't with her.

He was glad to be alone with Mae. Lillian was most likely already in bed. But Hannah, Mae's mother, could be nearby. She mostly stayed to herself in her bedroom when John visited, but he wasn't going to kiss Mae until he knew for sure.

"*Mamm* is already in her bedroom," Mae said as she grinned. "She said to tell you hello."

John rubbed his hands together to make sure they were warm enough, then wasted no more time before he cupped Mae's cheeks, his eyes fixed on hers. Could she read his expression? Did she know how much he loved her? They hadn't said the words, but he could feel the intensity of her emotions when he covered her mouth with his in a kiss that always left him weak in the knees.

Tonight was the night . . . that John would tell Mae that he was in love with her.

MAE WAS LOST in the euphoria of John's tender embrace, the way he held her face in his strong hands, and the exploratory way that he kissed her repeatedly. The crackling of the fire fueled the warmth in her heart, and she wished she could live in this moment forever.

Because it couldn't last.

She loved him so much it hurt sometimes, and when she wasn't with him, she longed to see him. It was a cross between agony and euphoria She was pretty sure he felt the same way but admitting it to each other would change things. It would feel like a commitment. Maybe they were already emotionally committed but saying it aloud would solidify a future that Mae could only dream about.

She eased out of his arms, kissed him tenderly on the cheek, then nodded to the coffee table. "I've got hot cider and cinnamon rolls."

"Those look delicious. And the decorations are beautiful too."

"*Danki*. Now let's get some food in you."

On the nights he visited her, he confessed to missing supper with his family, saying he was anxious to get on the road to see her. Most of the Amish families Mae knew, hers included, ate their evening meal at five o'clock. She'd repeatedly asked him to come for supper and that they could eat later those nights. He insisted it would be too late for all of them to eat since he had to work until five. After traveling home and handling his chores, he didn't arrive at her house until almost seven, sometimes later. Mae had offered to heat up leftovers for him, also, but he said he just wanted to focus his attention solely on her. She always made sure to have plenty of snacks though.

After they were settled on the couch, he took a big bite of cinnamon roll. "These are the best I've ever had," he said after he'd swallowed.

Mae chuckled. "You say that about everything me or *Mamm* make for you to eat." She imagined all the meals they could share together if they were to get married and have a family, something she used to think she wanted.

When he rubbed his stomach and smiled, an indication he was full after eating four large cinnamon rolls, Mae picked up their plates. Sometimes, she had finger sandwiches or snacks, but John had a fondness for anything freshly baked and didn't mind having it for supper. It was a long ride for him to visit her, and she appreciated the fact he had repeatedly told her that he didn't mind making the journey. She at least wanted to make sure he left with a full tummy . . . even if it was cinnamon rolls or a finger food.

Her relationship with John had begun as a distraction for Mae. Not that she wasn't wildly attracted to him, but she'd feared the grief over losing her father would leave her never feeling happy again. No one could fill the void of losing her dad, but John provided her with an escape. She had never meant to fall in love with him.

She held her breath as the clock in the kitchen ticked, trying to hear if her mother was crying in the bedroom, but she probably wouldn't hear her from the kitchen. As badly as Mae felt, the loss of her father seemed to have paralyzed her mother emotionally, even though she tried not to show it in front of her daughters. In some ways, there was just a shell of her mother left, a woman who went through the life she was expected to live, but like a robot who didn't express emotion. It wasn't that Hannah King wasn't a good mother to her children, but she was absent. Gone. Like Mae and Lillian's father but in a different way.

She refocused on John when she rounded the corner and came back to the living room. Could he be any more handsome? His dark hair was cut in the traditional style. She'd heard the English call it a bowl cut but John's bangs were long and pushed to the side, and he had what the Amish called 'hat hair' from where his hat had been on his head all day. But it was his dark eyes that Mae could get lost in, and with only the light from the lantern and the glow of the fire, gold flecks twinkled in his brown eyes and grew brighter as he grew closer.

John Byler wasn't just handsome. He truly cared about people, and it showed in his everyday actions. Since Mae had been around him, she'd seen him carry an elderly English woman's bags to her car when she struggled with the weight of her purchases at the lumberyard. He'd given a homeless man twenty dollars after his friend advised him against it, saying the man might just use it to buy alcohol or drugs. John's response was, "Or food." Then he just smiled.

His tenderness extended much further than strangers and was apparent the most when he was around his loved ones. John had a large family, and Mae knew all of them since they attended the same worship services. She liked to think her people were good in nature overall, but John seemed to take his goodness to another level, and she loved that about him.

As he put an arm around her, snuggling closer, Mae wondered if her father would have approved of them being alone together in the living room. *Probably not.* But Mae suspected her mother would have convinced him that Mae was responsible and that John could be trusted.

Mae missed her mother.

In between snacking on cinnamon rolls and sipping cider, they chatted about their day. John had spent the afternoon doing inventory at the lumberyard, and Mae told him about her visit with her aunt and uncle. Then John became unusually quiet, wringing his hands together.

Slowly he turned to her, tucked a strand of loose hair

behind her ear, nuzzled her neck, then gently brushed his lips against hers before they locked eyes.

"I have something to tell you, Mae King." He kissed the tip of her nose, and Mae stopped breathing. If it was what she thought it would be, then their time together would be coming to an end soon. "I can't hold it in any longer," he said in a whisper, the fire continuing to crackle, the clock ticking louder in Mae's mind.

Please don't. He would expect her to say it back, and she couldn't.

He gently took her cheeks into his hands and gazed into her eyes. "Mae, I—"

She crushed her lips to his, causing their foreheads to knock together. Any discomfort from their heads bumping was quickly dissipating as Mae kissed him with all the passion she felt. Because she knew it would be the last time.

He eased her away and captured her eyes again as he tenderly clutched her shoulders. "Mae, I *lieb* you. I know we're young, and I know we've only been seeing each other for three months, but I am sure I am in *lieb* with you."

Mae chewed on her bottom lip as she avoided his eyes, casting them down as she reached up and twirled the string of her prayer covering. She couldn't ignore him, and when she finally looked into his eyes, she saw his fear . . . fear that she didn't feel the same way.

"*Danki*," she finally said barely above a whisper. "That's nice of you to say," she added when his jaw dropped slightly, his eyes searching hers.

She stood abruptly. "Uh, I think I hear Lillian awake in

her room. I should probably go check on her." It was a lie she would ask God to forgive later.

John slowly lifted himself from the couch and looped his thumbs beneath his suspenders. "*Ya*, I should probably go. It's getting late."

It wasn't late, and he didn't look at her as he moved toward the door and quickly dressed in his coat, hat, and gloves.

Mae could feel her heart cracking. But this was the kindest thing to do for John, to let him move on and fall in love with someone who wanted to have a life with him. He was right . . . they were young. They would both get over this even though the pain in Mae's chest felt unbearable, and she hoped she could hold off her tears until he was gone.

At the door, he kissed her on the cheek. "Bye, Mae."

"Bye," she mouthed, aware that no sound came out.

After the door between them closed, she pressed her head to the wood and laid her hands flat against the surface on either side of her head. She didn't want to cry, but tears spilled down her cheeks just the same.

Then she heard a familiar sound coming from her mother's bedroom. Quiet whimpering.

Mae wanted to burst through her mother's bedroom door, climb into bed with her, and hold her tightly, to comfort her. Maybe it should be the other way around, but as badly as Mae was hurting, it was worse for her mother. Mae was never going to allow herself to love the way her mother had loved her father. She'd never survive the pain if she lost a husband, and she'd end up in constant agony like her mother.

She padded up the stairs, stopping to check on Lillian who was sound asleep, then she ran to her room and waited until she was behind her bedroom door before she pressed her face into her pillow and sobbed.

FINISH READING An Amish Christmas Gift on Amazon.

AMISH RECIPES

CATHERINE'S MEATLOAF

Ingredients:

2 pounds ground beef

1 small minced onion

2 eggs

3/4 cup bread crumbs

3/4 cup ketchup (divided)

2 tablespoons Worcestershire sauce

salt & pepper to taste

Instructions:

Preheat oven to 350 degrees. Line a baking sheet with foil.

Combine beef, onion, eggs, bread crumbs, ½ cup ketchup, Worcestershire sauce, 1 teaspoon salt, and ½ teaspoon pepper using a mixer or in a large bowl by hand. Mix until combined.

Rinse a 9x5" loaf pan with water (to help meatloaf release). Pack the meat mixture tightly in to the pan.

Flip the pan over the prepared baking sheet and jiggle carefully until the meatloaf slides out. Bake for 60 minutes.

Remove from oven. Increase oven temperature to 400 degrees. Brush remaining ¼ cup ketchup on all sides of the meatloaf. Return to oven and bake 10 minutes longer. Remove from oven and cool 15-20 minutes before serving.

LEMON SNOWFLAKE COOKIES

Ingredients:
    1 box lemon cake mix
    8 oz Cool Whip
    1 egg
    1/2 cup powdered sugar

Instructions:
    Combine all ingredients except the powdered sugar. Blend completely and refrigerate for 1 hour.

Preheat oven to 350 °F. Grease baking sheets or line with parchment paper. Put powdered sugar in a bowl. Drop batter by tablespoons into the powdered sugar and gently roll until covered.

Bake 12-14 minutes. Let them cool on the cookie sheet.

Store in air-tight container. Makes 36 cookies.

AMISH MOCHA BROWNIE DESSERT

Ingredients:

Brownie Layer:
 1 package chocolate cake mix
 3/4 cup cold butter
 1 egg, slightly beaten

Filling:
 8 oz. Cream cheese
 1 cup whipped topping
 1 cup powered sugar

Pudding:
 1 package chocolate pudding, instant
 1 package vanilla pudding, instant
 3 cups milk
 1 teaspoon instant coffee (optional)
 3 cups whipped topping
 chocolate shavings (optional)

Instructions:

In a large bowl, cut butter into cake mix until mixture looks like coarse crumbs.

Add egg and mix well.

Press into a 9x13 greased cake pan. Bake for 15-20 minutes at 350 until set.

Beat powered sugar and cream cheese, then fold in 1 cup whipped topping.

Spread over cooled crust, then refrigerate until set. In a bowl whisk together milk and both puddings.

Let stand for 5 minutes until slightly thickened.

Top with 3 cups whipped toppings.
Sprinkle chocolate shavings on top.
Place in refrigerator for two hours
Goes well with ice cream!

.

PENNSYLVANIA DUTCH CHOW CHOW

Ingredients:

3 cups cauliflower florets, broken into small pieces

1 (10 oz) pkg. green beans, trimmed into 1-inch lengths

1 medium sweet onion, chopped

1 large red bell pepper, seeds removed and chopped

1 cup frozen (thawed) or fresh corn kernels

1 (15.5 oz) can kidney beans, drained and rinsed

4 cups apple cider vinegar

2 cups sugar

1 tbsp kosher salt

1 tsp celery seed

1 tsp mustard seeds

1/2 tsp turmeric

Instructions:

Heat a large pot of water to a boil on high. Add the cauliflower and green beans. Cook until crisp-tender, 4-5 minutes. Drain and add to a large heatproof bowl with the onion, bell pepper, corn, and kidney beans.

In the same pot on medium-high, heat the vinegar, sugar, salt, celery seeds, mustard seeds, and turmeric. Simmer 5 min., stirring occasionally, until sugar and salt are dissolved.

To pot, add the vegetables, cover, return to a simmer, and cook 10 min. Pack into 2–3 quart-size canning jars and seal with clean lids. Allow jars to cool on a rack for 15 min., then refrigerate for up to 1 month.

ACKNOWLEDGMENTS

It takes a village to get a book out into the world—and the grace of God.

I'm often asked if I ever have writer's block, and the answer is "never". I've been writing stories in some capacity since I was a child. I knew it was my calling early on. But, without so many creative people in my court, it would be impossible to get my books in front of readers.

I have fabulous editors. Thank you to Audrey Wick and Janet Murphy for your continued keen insight, wisdom, and thoughtful encouragement. I'm incredibly grateful, and I love you both dearly.

A big thanks to Wiseman's Warriors, my street team. You gals continue to rock along with me on this wonderful journey. I appreciate everything you do to market my books, your input on covers, and your friendships.

To my husband, Patrick, sometimes it's a rollercoaster ride, but I am happy to be sitting beside you and doing life

ACKNOWLEDGMENTS

together. Thank you for all you do, not just for me, but for our entire family.

Much thanks to the rest of my family and friends. When this began, I don't think any of us thought I would write over sixty books. I'm blessed to have you on this journey for the long haul. Love each and every one of you.

And last, but never least, I raise up an abundant amount of thanks and praise to God.

ABOUT THE AUTHOR

Bestselling and award-winning author Beth Wiseman has sold over 3 million books. She is the recipient of the coveted Holt Medallion, a two-time Carol Award winner, and has won the Inspirational Reader's Choice Award three times. Her books have been on various bestseller lists, including CBD, CBA, ECPA, and *Publishers Weekly*. Beth and her husband are empty nesters enjoying country life in south central Texas.

Made in the USA
Monee, IL
05 January 2025

76184093R00132